# the philosophy

# of

# Peace

A Peace Series Novella

Jennifer Fisch-Ferguson

The Philosophy of Peace

Cover Design Credits: Tri-Crescent Photography – www.tri-crescent.com

Editor: J. Arthur's Writing Services – JAEdits.com

Copyright © 2017 Jennifer Fisch-Ferguson

ISBN: 978-1-945642-10-4

## Table of Contents

# Chapter One

Lauren Stage looked down at the glaring orange engine light and bit her bottom lip to keep from crying. She was already exhausted from her extremely early – or maybe super late—red- eye flight, and lack of a decent meal. Being broken down in the middle of god-knows-where Montana of all places didn't help her mood. According to her last glimpse at the GPS directions, she was still at least two hours away from Cascade. She had gotten off the highway with the promise of a gas station on the exit sign. She'd still had a quarter full tank a few hours ago, and the allure of a cold caffeinated beverage had also called to her. She hadn't anticipated getting any real sleep until later that night when properly settled in her hotel. Of course at this point it didn't look like any sleep would be fulfilled anytime soon.

"This is where ambition gets you. Stuck on the side of the road, probably because my idea of near-by is very different than the sign makers," she groused and then berated her past self. "Sure, I'll go to Montana and write a book about my ancestors. No problem, Dean Tol, I can research and write a book over the summer. No big deal, I'm at the end of the tenure track journey, this is what we do. Take the cheaper red-eye? Why not? I've got to learn to say 'No' darn quick. "

As an academic Lauren always thought her life would be inspiring the young and impressionable minds of the future. She would help them expand their knowledge base, all the while encouraging them to take risks to think more broadly and analyze everything. Which she did; alongside committee meetings, teaching classes, and the pressure of publishing scholarly articles or books every year. She'd been building an impressive CV for the last five years just to make sure nothing would go wrong, and now it was time to pull out all stops. Getting tenure not only wasn't necessarily easy, it was nerve wracking.

"All I had to do is put my life on display for a group of people to judge and decide if I am good enough," she muttered, watching the needle on the gas gauge dip past empty. "I know this book is the finishing piece and will help, but holy damn! I kind of thought the rat race would've ended once I got my doctorate. You know, being a professional and expert and all."

Her mentor, Vince, had pressed her into the trip. Of course the study grant hadn't hurt either. She'd asked for and received full funding to spend the summer researching black cowboys, mainly those from her family line. She chuckled and snorted when she thought about it. It seemed kind of silly, but she was a cultural rhetorician, not to mention getting paid to study her family line was the type of thing others would be jealous about. The prospect of the trip had seemed immensely exciting, of course that was before she got stranded on the side of the road. The drive had been moving along by just fine, when she took the exit she figured it would be a quick stop to stretch her legs and shake off some driving fog.

Long past the point where she could see the exit, and before she could see the gas station, she felt the car shudder a bit. She figured she'd run over some road kill, and didn't pay any mind until the car sputtered a few times more. She looked at the gas meter and noticed she'd had less fuel than she thought. As she'd pulled over to the side of the road, there were shudders, clunks and a few hisses from the car and then it just stopped. The engine did turn over, so she'd stayed put while trying to put together a rescue plan. But of course while she sat there, inspiration had hit for a chapter on making ties from the past for future connections. Ignoring the outside world for hours, she'd worked non-stop on the chapter before she lost her words. The battery on her laptop dying forced her to stop her work. To her surprise, she found the car silent. Meaning the engine had stopped, and when she checked, the gas needle was buried past empty. Which meant she would have to deal with her problem of not having a working vehicle.

Looking at the inky blackness of the road before her and then back to her no-service having cell phone, she sighed. The entire time she'd been working, no other vehicles had passed by and it had been hours. She was pretty certain the exit must have a curse or something the locals knew to avoid. Her watch read almost half past four in the morning. Rather than become the victim of whatever slasher movie demon would come and get her, Lauren locked the car door, and then relocked it five times just to make sure and snuggled in to take a nap until the sun rose.

"Ohmygosh," Lauren shrieked and then mean mugged the jeep and its driver from her rearview mirror. "Did I really say that out loud? I can't believe I've picked up my students' lingo. I can't believe he just honked at me like that. Not like he can't drive around."

She watched a tall man, wearing cowboy boots, jeans, a light gray t-shirt with the UConn mascot on the front, and an honest to goodness cowboy hat approach her car. He was beautiful to look at; a fluid walking motion captured her attention all the way up to her window. Lauren noticed his wide sable colored eyes and felt heat curl around in her stomach like a contented cat. He smiled down at her and she continued her perusal. His skin was tan from being in the sun, and a light dusting of stubble covered his face. Blond hair was tucked neatly under his hat, but a few curls escaped at his temple and she wondered if they would be soft to her touch. As his smile faltered, Lauren wondered what was wrong, until he knocked on the window.

"Right," she muttered.

Heat suffused her face as she pushed the button for the window. No gas meant no power to the engine. She cracked the door open and smiled. He looked more like a model than a cowboy.

"Hi, there. Can I help you?"

The soft voice shattered Lauren's idea of what a cowboy should sound like. No slang in the whole five words he had used. Again she stared until he cleared his throat. She prayed he wouldn't think her an idiot and forced her brain to work enough to form a sentence.

"My rental car is broken," she said lamely. "And I don't have any cell service. Can I borrow your phone to call for some help, please?"

"Sure. Although a better plan might be for me just to help you out, not just offer my phone. I have a tow rope in the back of my jeep. I'm happy to take you into Peace," he said. "I'm Jared."

# The Philosophy of Peace

Lauren stared at him again, hoping Peace was the name of the town and not some lame pick up line. She tilted her head up to look at him, and caught the amused grin creasing his lips. She snuck a quick look into the mirror, to make sure she didn't look a mess. Her mocha skin was carried a slight blush from being scared, at least that's what she sold herself. Her natural auburn-brown hair was still up in a messy bun with her natural curls almost behaving. Her standard business casual slacks and blouse were fairly wrinkle free, at least enough to be presentable. She turned her hazel eyes back to meet his brown and smiled.

"Thank you. A tow into town sounds great," she said.

"Okay, let me get in position and we can get you all fixed up," Jared said.

Not sure what she should be doing, Lauren sat in the car while Jared backed the tuck in front of the car. She watched him walk in between the slim space between the vehicles and strained to see as he bent in from of the bumper. Not that she minded the view as she got a clear view of his backside in form fitting jeans. Interviewing real life cowboys for her story took an appealing turn. She got out of the car when he motioned to her and watched as he attached a rope to the bumper of the vehicle by looping it and made sure it wouldn't come loose.

"You need to make sure you attach the rope to the frame of a car. That way you don't pull off the bumper," he said, breaking the silence while he worked.

"This is good to know," she said with a laugh. "Especially since I never plan to ever tow anything."

"Noted," Jared said. "If your car still has battery power, you need to turn on your flashers. I'll also my use flashers. This lets everyone know I'm towing you even if they can't see the rope. Go ahead and put the car in the neutral position. This should be quick and easy. Dunn's should be able to fix you up."

Lauren walked back to the car, leaned in and grabbed her work bag; it looked like she would have some premium writing time once she got to the town. She had no idea what was wrong with the stupid car. She just hoped it would be a quick fix and she wouldn't lose the interview time with the library's archivist that had taken her four months to arrange.

"The battery is dead," she said. "I tried it a million times before you came. I don't think the flashers will work."

Jared held the door open for her and she gratefully climbed up into the jeep, as gracefully as she could. The ride toward town was silent and she realized all his walk-through instructions had been an attempt to calm her down. She had nothing to say and her rescuer didn't seem to have the need to fill the space with idle chatter. They drove through impressive farm land with picturesque mountains as a backdrop. She craned her neck to watch as they passed a wide open field where cattle were being guided by men on horseback. As they came closer to the town, Lauren swallowed a heavy sigh. If the place had internet she would be surprised. The last time she had been in Montana she'd been presenting at a university, where the people were.

"Dunn's Auto Body is a decent shop," Jared said. "If you want I can drop you off at Sheila's diner while you wait."

"Thank you," Lauren said. "Is there a hotel or anything? In case I have to make an extended stay? Or better yet, there doesn't happen to be a *Get-Up-and-Go* rental center nearby?"

"I've never heard of that particular car rental place anywhere. But the guys at the shop are honest and quick. There is a bed and breakfast close by in town in case you have to stay."

"What's the point of using a national car rental if they aren't everywhere," she sighed.

The husky chuckle made her stomach do the flip-flop thing it had earlier. She stared straight ahead, afraid she would blush again if she caught him looking at her. The last ten minutes were spent in calm silence. As promised, the car was dropped off at Dunn's and Jared even walked her in to the diner. Lauren felt her throat constrict as all heads turned when they walked in.

"Hi Jared," a petite waitress said. "Two?"

"Just one, Sheila junior, I'm just making sure the lady gets settled."

"I swear I'm going to salt your lemonade if you call me that again," the waitress said with a roll of her eyes. "Surely someone like you can manage to pronounce the name Crystal."

"Just be nice to Lauren," Jared said as he walked back out the door. "Bye, junior."

"Can I buy you a cup of coffee or something?" Lauren said hastily, not willing to be left alone just yet.

"Sorry, I need to get back to work," he said over his shoulder. "You're in good hands."

Lauren followed the waitress and sat in a corner booth. The waitress handed her the menu, sat across from, and gave her a wide grin.

"So, he rescued you, huh?"

Lauren tried to ignore the popping gum sound.

"Yes, my car broke down," she offered and kept speaking to drown out the sound. "He said the name of the town is Peace? How far from Cascade are we?"

"We're in the middle of nowhere. About three hours from Cascade, unless you drive like me then you can make it in two," the young woman laughed. "How about lemonade, I promise I won't salt it."

"Lemonade sounds great," Lauren laughed.

Crystal stood up and bounced over to the drink dispenser. Lauren wasted no time and pulled out her laptop and after a few moments under the booth found an outlet. She waited for it to boot up so she could be efficient. There was no reason not to get some work done while she was stranded. Crystal brought out a glass of lemonade and waited for her to take a sip. It might have been the trauma of travel, or the heat the day had already shown, but the drink satisfied Lauren in a way she hadn't known possible.

"Good, right?" the waitress smiled. "What else can I get you? The pancakes are good."

"For lunch?" Lauren asked.

"Definitely. Let me recommend the BLT pancakes with chipotle mayo."

"Sure, let's do that."

A few moments later Crystal returned with her food, and once again sat in the booth with Lauren.

"Why'd you come to Peace?"

*Okay, so it is the name of the town.*

"Other than open dusty ranch space, there's nothing interesting here. Unless you count the Founder's Day celebration. But that's not for a week or so," Crystal said, still chomping away.

"I'm doing some research," Lauren said between bites of the best pancakes she'd ever had.

"On what?"

"African American cowboys. One my of my elders was the first female cowhand up in Cascade."

"Ahhhh, Mary. That's a good story," Crystal nodded. "You know, you should probably talk to some of the men around here. They come from some pretty long lines of cowboys. They might be a bit shy about talking to you, so ask Jared to introduce you."

Lauren didn't miss the look on Crystal's face and ate the last, too big bite, to hide the smile. She knew how the girl felt; the man was delicious to look at. However, she wouldn't be there long and didn't need to have gossip going around about her. After her lunch, Crystal directed her over to the only bed and breakfast the town had. She rented the last available room and sighed in relief when given the internet password. Lauren walked into her room at the B&B and looked around. It was a bright and spacious room decorated in soft mauve, green and rose. It had four windows, three of which form a large bay embracing a luxurious looking bed. In addition there was a desk for her to work at and a cushy sofa that she could imagine curling up on to read her notes.

Before all of those plans, though, she needed a shower. After the long flight and night in her car, she wanted to wash the bad start off of her and try again. The hot water beat against her skin and relaxed her. The homemade lavender soap was amazing in scent and silky feeling. She reluctantly left the shower and curled up on the sofa to read her notes, but instead drifted off in exhaustion.

# Chapter Two

When Lauren woke, she groaned. The clock on the bed stand read almost nine, and with the streams of light pouring in through the window, she knew she's slept almost a full day. She sat up and regretted the action as her sleep hangover spun her vision around. No doubt she'd needed the rest after all of the excitement of her travel. For once she forced herself to move slowly. She took the longest, hottest shower she could, the homemade soap smelled amazing. She let her thoughts ramble all over until her fingers felt pruney. After a liberal application of lotion and body spray, Lauren twisted her hair into a top knot. For a moment she thought about putting on some make-up, but decided to go with mascara only. Even though she was working, she wasn't at work and decided to go with her natural looks. She pulled out slacks and another blouse and shrugged, she would be over dressed, she knew but there were no other options unless she wanted to go shopping. Which she didn't.

She walked down the stairs and reveled in the quiet of being alone. Her fear about staying in a bed and breakfast and having forced interactions abated. She smiled at the note she found on the kitchen counter directing her where to find her food. Along with a bowl of fresh fruit and a carafe of coffee; a delicious stack of French toast waited for her. It had been a long time since she'd had anything other than a cup of coffee for breakfast and she had no shame when her mouth really watered. Lauren took her breakfast back up to her room, and sat on the comfy sofa. She turned to look out the large window and people watched. Across the town she could see the hustle and bustle of daily small town life. Unlike Maryland, people often stopped to talk on the street, and no car horns blaring. She set the empty dishes aside and grabbed her notes. Despite having a top of the line laptop, Lauren always took notes by hand. Not only soothing, she loved the tactile feel of a smooth pen sliding across paper. While she loved history, somehow she'd never really imagined she would have anything to do with cowboys.

With her studies and classes she often looked at and discussed the history of the African American experience as entrepreneurs after the Civil War, but never once had thought about anything other than blue collar industries. She knew African American cowboys must have existed, but since she'd never really thought about it, she'd been amazed at she'd been finding about their long and rich history. What Lauren had found in her current research showed centuries of law men, law breakers, and cowboys way beyond the well-known "Buffalo Soldiers", and even more importantly how the wide open nature of the West had lent to a less discriminatory nature.

"Sure," she said to herself with a small grin. "It's rather had to be racist in the middle of a stampede. Not like the cows were going to trample the white cowhands less than the black. I'm pretty sure trampling included everyone."

During her research she found that after the Civil War, a cowboy was in high demand because of the skills the men had learned while being used as slave labor. Lauren scribbled down more notes about the hardships the men had still gone through as they travels through towns, on cattle runs, like not being able to stay at hotels or eat at public restaurants. Her phone rang and shocked her out of her writing haze. She smiled down at the extra pages of notes, happy with her progress when Dunn's called and asked her to come down and discuss her car.

She nearly gagged as a wave of heat hit her as she walked out the door. July had some nerve being so hot, considering how Montana was much further up north. Now, if she'd been back in Maryland, she would've expected the staggering temperatures. Somehow she'd convinced herself Montana wouldn't be as hot as... well she hadn't thought much about it at all, as the deadlines from her work had consumed her. Ten minutes later, she walked into the shop and made it a point not to rush to the water cooler and drink all five gallons.

"Ms. Stage, nice to meet you."

"Mr. Dunn," she greeted.

"Oh naw, ma'am. That's my father. You can call me Foster,"

"Okay, please call me Lauren."

"Right then, Lauren. Let's talk about this car of yours. Tell me what happened."

Thirty minutes later, she waited to hear her verdict. She had told Foster all about the low gas, then running over something, and how the car wouldn't start after that. She never considered running over and object could rip open her fuel line or gas tank.

"Well, Lauren, you ran out of gas so quickly because the rubber cap attached to the gas tank developed a crack after you hit the mystery item. We might have a small problem," Foster drawled. "I need to make a few phone calls. Can you hang out for a few moments?"

She nodded and gave a rueful smile. Of course she would have a problem. So far the whole trip had been full of them, and she was on day two. She sat on the world's most uncomfortable chair and pulled out her notes. To pass the time as she walked, she mentally categorized the information she had been researching to tell about her ancestor Mary Fields. After all, if the woman would've stayed in Tennessee where she'd been born, Lauren wouldn't have been stuck half way across the country, stranded and trying to find some help. But her ancestor made for a great story; one that almost sounded completely made up. Amazing was way too weak of a compliment for such a complete bad-ass.

"Stagecoach" Mary Fields had a life most people couldn't have survived; yet she managed to do so for almost one hundred years, and decades later it kept people in awe. The best part - at eighty-two years old and in the early 1900's, she had owned a saloon; better yet she made standing bet for anyone crazy enough to try it out. She had promised for five hard earned dollars and a glass of her best whiskey, she could knock out any cowboy in Cascade, Montana with a single punch. Only four men were stupid enough to take her up on it. After her fourth and final victory, nobody ever had the balls to challenge her again.

That little tidbit would make for a pretty awesome opening to the first chapter, and Lauren grinned as she thought about a woman so strong she made her own rules in a time where she shouldn't have had any power. In moments of crazy, like the one she was in, it helped to know she came from hearty stock. She continued reviewing her notes and shaking her head at all the woman had been able to accomplish, despite hefty odds. Idly she also wondered what the rule was on using the f-bomb in an academic text. She just didn't see how she could talk about the woman without a few cuss words. Mary was a mysterious, don't-ever- mess- with-me woman too smart to leave a clear trail about her true background; the best estimate of her birthdate had been guessed at on or around 1832, but no one knew. Lauren figured peppering in little tidbits about Mary's past would keep the pace of the story moving along. Mary had escaped from Tennessee and worked her way across the country. Despite the birth date being nebulous, she was fond of celebrating, and because she'd such an impact with the good people of Cascade, Montana, the town had made it a point to closed all the businesses twice a year to celebrate both of her claimed birthdays, mostly because she told them to.

Lauren chuckled at the thought. Who would've thought a runaway slave could have done the amazing things she had done? Maybe she would be better off on in the world of academia if she acted more like Mary –she'd just have to become a hard smoking, hard drinking, and hard swearing rebellious woman with a penchant for tall tales. Heck, she already was an amazing story teller; her master's degree had focused on folks tales as means of passing family history. She could focus on spinning the already hard to believe stories into the tales of a legendary figure from history. She could set up a rich history full of allegorical details to tell about Mary's time working on a Mississippi steamboat. Showing how this six-foot tall, two hundred pound powerhouse of a woman rolled from the mighty river all the way into the rough-and-tumble frontier town would set the scene. When people got skeptical and needed more examples, Lauren could launch into the tale of Mary with a six-shooter and a flask of whiskey in her work apron, and a home-rolled cigar clenched between her teeth, just daring anyone to give her a funny look. Mary's enduring legend would ensure the woman cowboy could live on in fame as the amazing woman who helped to forge the Great American West.

Foster walked up to her and seeing the look on his face, Lauren pulled Mary's energy around her, ready to hear the worst.

"The bad news is that we don't have your particular cap on hand," Foster said. "The good news is there is one at the auto parts store a few hours away. I planned to go there tonight after closing to get others parts. It looks like you will get to spend one more night here."

"I don't suppose there is a car rental place there?"

Lauren knew she sounded desperately hopeful but didn't crumple when he shook his head 'no'. A buzzer sounding as the front door opened interrupted her thoughts. The perfect silhouette of a cowboy entered the repair shop with the sun at his back.

"Hey Foster, can you pick up that windshield rest hood bumper when you go get those parts today? And I need…"

Lauren recognized Jared's voice before he actually came into view. He still looked good to her, despite the light coating of dust. She forced her hand to stay at her side instead of giving him a little wave.

"Sure thing. You got the model number?"

Unsure if she should greet him or just stay quiet, she stood there while the men talked. Lauren wasn't sure if Foster was done talking to her about the car, or what. She hated instances like this where she didn't know what she should be doing. She bit her bottom lip, waiting for a pause in the conversation.

"Hi, Lauren."

She looked up and met Jared's eyes.

"Crystal told me you might be able to lead me to some African American cowboys who are generational here."

Amazingly she did not combust or die from mortification as she blurted out randomness instead of a greeting. Neither man laughed at her, but Foster did nod and walk back behind the counter.

"Hi, Lauren," Jared said again.

"Hi, Jared," she said.

She couldn't quite read him, but stiffened up at because he seemed to be correcting her. She'd spent too much time being corrected. She continued with the question she had.

"Was Crystal just trying to keep me talking, or is she on target?"

He laughed and Lauren waited for him to make eye contact again. No way was she going to apologize for asking her question. She'd spent most of her career defending every idea she had, and she had grown a spine.

"Crystal is correct. I do work with a lot of generational cowboys. If you give me a day I'm sure I can arrange a few people to talk with you."

"Okay," she said. "It doesn't look like I'm going anywhere any time soon. I probably should've gone with a larger car chain."

"Or not run over random pieces of roadkill," Foster grinned at her.

"Well, if you want to be particular," Lauren said. "I'd rather blame the car company. I mean, who makes a gas tank that is so delicate a bitty piece of dead rabbit breaks it?"

Both men nodded, and she sighed in relief. It had all be in fun. Sometimes she couldn't tell if she read situations wrong. Often she felt she had to be on guard, she didn't have a bunch of experience dating, so interacting men could be hazardous. These men, however, seemed to be waiting for her to say her piece. The lack of condescending tones and looks were nice. They also didn't seem bothered by long pauses in conversation. Lauren however became more and more unnerved as the silence carried on. Foster nodded and slipped back behind the counter. She watched him leave and tried to figure out how to continue the conversation.

"This is true; cars should be made tougher stuff. You're in good hands though. The Dunn's are the best at what they do," Jared interrupted her thoughts. "How was the B&B?"

Grateful for the nice safe topic she answered without putting her thoughts in order.

"Lovely, I had the best French toast in the world this morning. Thanks again for the ride. Can I buy you dinner tonight?"

There it was-- her awkward out in full display. His slight pause made her nervous.

"Excuse me," Foster said. "Jared, those Rock Crawler corner guards you ordered came in last night. Want to come check them out?"

Lauren felt deflated as the men walked away from her and behind the counter. Her car was broken, research delayed for at least one more day, and she hadn't gotten an answer to her impromptu dinner offer.

*Did he think I asked him on a date? I just wanted to repay him for... well scaring the crap out of me, but also bringing me into town. I guess I am done here? Not like the town is big, they know where I am staying.*

She packed up her notes. She turned to say good-bye, but the men were nowhere to be seen. Lauren, nodded to no one, and exited. She'd almost made it back to the B&B before she heard her name called out. She turned to find Jared walking, no strolling, toward her. Granted his long legs covered the distance between them in just a few seconds.

"Lauren?"

"Jared?"

"You left before I answered your question," he said with an easy smile.

"Well, you guys seemed all wrapped up in those corner guards," she said. "I didn't want to break in on your squee fest."

She swore he was biting back a laugh.

"We don't squee over jeep parts," he said.

"The sounds might not have been made, but you two were definitely in squee mode," she said.

Lauren looked up at him, amusement covering her face, while she watched his face go through possible answers to give her back.

"Yes, I will have dinner with you. Tonight I already have plans, so it will have to be later. Be ready at seven tomorrow night. I'll pick you up," Jared said. "We will have to continue our discussion about this so-called squee'ing. Meanwhile I am needed at the ranch."

Lauren managed a dignified nod and made it to her room at the B&B before she broke into laughter.

# Chapter Three

Lauren felt a sense of victory in having her car back. Sure the crappy little rental still rumbled along, but it worked. True to his promise, Jared had called her at the bed and breakfast to give her the names of half a dozen men who were generational cowboys willing to speak with her. They'd offer to chat with her after dinner time the next day, the bulk of their work would be done and they set aside time to talk with her. It left her all day to pace in her room while she checked and triple checked her notes and questions. While she hoped the conversation would naturally open up beyond the questions, she made sure to have enough to keep the talks going.

A few rattles from the car brought her attention back to her surroundings. Because of the low light of dusk, Lauren couldn't see much down the dusty road, not cows and she'd expected a lot of them. She followed Jared's directions carefully; the road markers were pretty faded and didn't show up often. When she questioned why she was meeting out on the grounds instead of the at the ranch headquarters, Jared told her the men were out with the cattle and said it would be easier for her to meet them out there. She drove for about ninety minutes, reviewing the questions she wanted to ask. She knew the Montana census showed the past diverse occupations for its African American residents; everything from laborers, cooks and most surprising a good deal of barbers. She had expected more of them would have worked for others, but there were a good deal of small business owners catering to their own community. The next biggest populations in the area were the cowboys, ranch hands and miners, even though there was plenty of experience on running ranches, not as many men had the money to start their own. The African American population continued to grow because of the steamboat travel and the employment opportunities offered. Lauren prayed family stories would fill in the missing details of the true experience.

She still felt like she had a lot to learn about the culture and society of the black residents. Despite having studied a lot about the history after the Civil War, this current research reminded her just how much she didn't know. Unlike the South, Montana hadn't posted signs to tell patrons who could come into restaurants and bars, but it was implicitly understood where residents were allowed to fraternize. The African American citizens came together and established their own churches, newspapers, and social clubs, and were just as limiting to outsider access. She looked forward to talking to the men about what their family had been through and how the communities were shaped and changed. She squinted as shapes in the distance became distinctly more cow and man shaped. Putting a smile on her face, Lauren kept it there until she relaxed. By the time she reached the men, it was genuine.

Four hours later, a large bumping motion brought her out of her research contemplating drivers haze. She had been in the speculation zone about the stories she had heard during her amazing chance at interviews. She slowed the car to listen better, but didn't stop. It seemed to be running okay and she still had at least twenty minutes to drive to even find a main road. And in just a short ten minutes later, Lauren once again found herself in her non-working rental car. She wanted to scream and cry, but more importantly she just wanted to get back to Peace. All she wanted was hot date with her laptop to transcribe all of her notes and flush out her book.

The cool evening offered the only blessing of the moment. The semi-darkness swallowed all the defining details around her, but Lauren stopped and looked for something that might tell her where she was. Nothing but dry, dusty land greeted her, no road signs to be found. She took a deep wavering breath, but refused to cry because it would cost her body moisture. The sun had set about two minutes before, but the heat surrounded her and Lauren scowled. She refused to give in to panic, she just needed to get her head together and make a plan. She figured she could just go ahead and sit in the car until the morning. Again. The cowboys should be back at dawn and find her. Or, she could probably walk the few miles and get to the busier cross road. She began to calculate where she should be after having driven for about seventy minutes. She turned in a slow circle looking around at empty land. Digging into her pocket, she pulled out her phone. It had two bars of battery and two bars of service, and yet when she tried to make a call nothing went through. However it was just enough to allow her to use the compass app.

Lauren reached into the car, to grab her precious notes. She didn't care if the car spontaneously burst into flame, but her work was important. She adjusted her work bag onto her left shoulder and began to walk. After a half hour the compass continued to point north, toward open land. She thought she would've been in town by now, but so far, nothing was even around. Even worse darkness had begun to set. Nothing like what she experienced in Maryland where city burn spilled light out everywhere. She knew she had to be close.

After twenty more minutes into her adventure, Lauren had given up. Somehow, she'd managed to get lost, walking in a straight line. The map app showed that she was right on the edge of town, but very dim open expanses of land were the only thing she saw when shining her phone around. Her legs refused to walk anymore, so she decided to wait until a better plan came to mind. A while later, found her sitting on the hard packed ground burning the outline of her story to keep the things that wanted to eat her away. She wasn't worried because an entire copy of the manuscript was up in the cloud, but the situation pissed her off. She only hoped for dawn to show before she had to burn her new notes. The rental car company would be getting her ire and then some. Lauren had given up hope. Hot, pissed off and scared out of her mind wasn't the best state to be tending a fire, but there she sat. At first, she had tried to figure out where she went wrong with the map. It took some time for her to recognize no cell signal, meant no internet, which meant no location finder. Essentially she'd been walking blindly the entire time. After one too many unidentifiable noises, she sat down, pulled out the pages and her lighter.

"Makes me wish I had taken up smoking," she muttered. "At least I would have something calming to do."

"I'm sure your lungs thank you for not assaulting them."

Lauren shrieked and hopped to her feet, only to whirl around and fall face first into the chest of the man who'd spoken behind her. She was fairly certain she would be dying at the hands of the stranger she just tripped into and screamed again. His chest muffled the sound. It took her a moment to realize that he stood there, quietly waiting for her to calm herself.

"You have good lungs I see," he said. "Smoking isn't your calling."

His laughter was a soft rumble against her cheek and she stood up straight. He was at least six inches taller than her five foot elven frame. Not many men she'd met were that much taller than her. The pitiful fire didn't cast much light, but there was enough to tell he grinned down at her.

"Jared?" she asked. "Why are you here?"

"Finding you," he said. "Why are you sitting out here? More importantly, why do you have a fire going out here? It's dangerous this time of year."

"I heard things," Lauren stuttered. "I didn't want them to get close, so I burned my book."

"You burned your book?"

"You know, the reason I needed those interviews? I'm writing a book on my ancestors who were cowboys here in Montana," she said. "Don't worry I have a backup."

"Ah, I figured you were doing a family tree. Instead I have an author on my hands. So then I can get a signed copy?"

"Uh, yeah. Okay."

She was thankful for the darkness of night. A scarlet blush had to be covering her face, as she noted her less than articulate answers. It didn't help that Jared gave her an understanding grin, moments before he kicked sand onto her small fire and put it out.

"What are you doing?" she gasped.

"Making sure random embers don't get caught on the wind and set the brush on fire and burn the farm down," he said simply. "Come on, I've got something to show you."

Lauren stood looking at him, and then drawing on some of Mary, put her hands on her hips.

"I'm not going anywhere with you. I don't even know who you are."

She blushed again; she hadn't meant to say something so stupid. Less than twenty-four hours ago she'd asked him to dinner as a thank you for giving her a ride. Now she resisted being alone with him. He clicked on a flash light and she could see him, well at least the part that wasn't covered in shadows.

"Well, darling..."

"Don't you call me darling," she insisted.

"You did ask me to dinner," he chuckled echoing her earlier thoughts. "Although, it would have been in town where there is a crowd of people. Okay, let's get to know each other. Do you want to ask the first question or should I?"

"I'll go," she said and scrunched her nose. She didn't plan to give him something easy after the second scare and embarrassing herself. "What song do you have completely memorized?"

"The Real Slim Shady."

"That doesn't count as a song," she protested.

"According to Billboard top 100 it is," Jared said smugly. "What's your claim to fame?"

*Aside from all my research articles?*

"I can count the number of words in any sentence while someone is talking and still pay attention to what the person is saying. You just said 12 words."

She watched as he mentally counted and grinned.

"Is it out of boredom?" he asked.

"Nope, just a quirk. I learn best aurally, and this is just natural. Though, I've been told it makes people anxious. What kind of art do you like best?"

"Portraits," he answered. "I just don't get abstract art. Splashes of paint on a canvas just look like splashes of paint. I'm sure the artist had rage or happiness or grief, but it still just looks like spatter. What's the best compliment you've ever received?"

She didn't even have to pause.

"Last year I was invited to perform at Diwali by my Bollywood teacher. She gave me five days to make up choreography and memorize it. That was a great compliment about her belief in my dance skills. Even better, after the performance, I got many compliments from many people about how authentic and emotional I made the dance look. What a great job I did honoring the intention of the song. Best night ever."

Lauren knew she had a huge grin. Even a year later, the memory still brought happiness. She'd always loved to dance, but being told she had nailed the song perfectly by the people in the culture had been better than the high of performing the dance.

"What was the song about?" Jared asked.

"A beautiful woman lets everyone know that she knows she's fabulous. A guy who likes her agrees and she agrees with him and flirts with him. Then she leaves and goes on her merry way," Lauren laughed. "My turn, If you had to change your name, what would you change it to?"

She caught a brief glance away, or at least she thought she did. Trying to read someone by flashlight wasn't easy.

"I've always liked…," he started to say.

Lauren cursed her overly loud and aggressive grumbling stomach. No, she hadn't had dinner, but the timing sucked. He gave her a grin, as if he dodged something. She wanted to know and began to ask the question again.

"Well, Lauren," he left a deliberate pause after letting her name fall from his lips like molasses. "How about we I make some dinner and you can tell me, how you managed to get stranded on the middle of the farm. I'm beginning to think the car has it out for you."

She nodded and watched Jared pick up half burned pages off the ground. He turned and began to walk.

"We're walking?"

"It's quick," he said.

"I guess that's why I didn't hear you drive up."

It seemed like only a few moments passed when they made it to a small cabin. No lights were on; if they had been she knew she would've seen them.

"No electricity?" she asked.

"I didn't have a chance to go in. From my porch I could see the fire you started. It looked too small to be a wild fire, but I had to check and make sure. A small fire easily escalates in the summer."

"You don't leave a light on for when you come home late?"

"Don't need to."

She waited for him to push the door open and turn on a light, and then peeked cautiously inside the cabin. It was simple; a small kitchen, a couch and two doors leading to what she assumed were the bedroom and bathroom. The decision to enter was decided by her nose. Something smelled great.

"So a campfire is bad, but leaving the stove on is fine?"

"Crockpot."

She rolled her eyes. Of course it would be a crockpot.

"Take the door on the left and freshen up. I'll get dinner ready," Jared said.

Lauren stared at herself in the mirror over the sink. Her mocha skin was a bit pale from stress and made the freckles across her cheeks stand out. Her hair looked like she had walked across the desert, so she pulled back into a neat, low bun. After a deep breath she opened the bathroom door.

"Wow. That smells great."

She once again got fuzzy feelings as Jared looked over his shoulder and smiled at her. Lauren sat on the couch, since it was the only seating option. She fidgeted while she waited. No one knew where she was. Actually the sad fact was that no one was expecting her to call and check in. Other than an ex-boyfriend, she had no one to check in with. Well, there was Vince, but their relationship didn't really extend outside work. Then again, the man had done nothing but help her out. She wasn't sure if she was afraid of him or the fact that she thought she might have feelings for him.

"Dinner?"

Lauren startled but didn't shriek this time. Mostly because she'd managed to doze off and his touch on her shoulder had been gentle. Jared placed two plates on a trunk and pulled it in front of the couch. A huge burger, crisp green beans and apple slices enticed her.

"Sorry to wake you," he said. "But you do need to eat dinner."

"This looks great. And you move quietly. If you stomped about, I would hear you and probably not get startled."

"Hope you like bison."

Lauren's head snapped up and her eyes met his. There was no way he could possibly know.

"What?"

"Bison burger."

"You cook burgers in a crockpot? Why am I not surprised. I had no idea you could make anything but stew in a crockpot."

Without hesitation she picked up the burger and took a bite. Lauren wanted to laugh at herself when she actually closed her eyes in enjoyment. With no shame, she dug in and in short time finished her meal.

"Without a doubt, you're an amazing cook. It wasn't overcooked at all," she said, sitting back. "What's your secret?"

"Daily practice," he said with a smile. "For a second there I thought you were going to refuse it."

"No way. Avocado bison burgers are my favorite back home. Except your burger is the best I've had."

"Fresh makes a difference."

Silence fell between them. Lauren couldn't think of anything to say, mostly from exhaustion. She leaned back full and content.

"How about you take my bed? I'll take you to town in the morning. It's over and hour ride and you look exhausted"

Lauren realized she had dozed off on the couch. Again.

"I can just sleep here," she said.

"I figured you'd want a door to close," Jared said.

"Do you snore or something?" she grinned.

"We're still getting to know each other."

She loved the sound of his laughter; rich and homey. Through half lidded eyes she studied him. His skin had probably been olive hued before its exposure to the sun, but he wore his tan well.

# The Philosophy of Peace

His eyes were a pretty brown she could fall into and he had laugh lines around his mouth. His hair was shorter than it had been a few days ago; she missed the curls.

"I'm sure I can trust you. Besides it's your bed and you need more sleep than I do."

"Probably," he said. "But I figured you'd want some privacy."

She shrugged and stood up. There was no good for reason her not to accept his generous offer. She did admit to her ever flipping trust of him, and realized she must already trust him. Sleep reclaimed her the moment her head hit the pillow.

# Chapter Four

The crack of the whip pushed the horses to run harder and faster. If they stopped, they could be dead, although the weather seemed not to care about their impending doom. The stagecoach creaked as it listed side to side its nuts and bolts complaining about the abuse. The inky dark night offered only another challenge as the terrain was rough and uncertain. But it didn't matter, there was a job to do and it was necessary. The food and medicine carefully packed for St. Pete's mission had to be delivered before any more of the precious children succumbed to disease and illness. A bone chilling howl cut through the air, prompting Mary to push the now frantic animals to their limit. It wasn't enough to deter the hunger of starving wolves. She turned her head to size up her challenge. The wolves had been trailing her for miles, assessing them as prey and looking for any signs of weakness. She knew what the wolves lack in size, they would make up in collaboration and cunningness. The horses' nostrils gave out huge plumes of smoke, betraying their effort and fatigue.

One of the horses stumbled and the whole team was thrown off. Mary struggled to control the panicked animals and the coach, but it flipped over. Jumping out of the way of the falling death trap, Mary grabbed her knife and cut the horses out of their tethers to give them a fighting chance as the pack rounded in on them to attack. Twelve large gray wolves charged in, spooking some horses into running and launching attacks designed to rip up the animals injured from the cart flipping over. Mary used the overturned structure to help shield her back. She carefully lit a small lamp and surveyed the scene. Two horses lay dead with the ferocious wolves taking down the last remaining one. Then they turned toward her. The first wolf went down with a fiery blast from her shot gun; too close of range for her taste.

Through the rest of the night Mary stayed awake and warm by pacing behind the fallen stagecoach. She periodically let off a shot to remind the wolves not to stray to close. Around dawn the next day she'd switched to her revolver because she'd run out of buckshot. When the sun finally rose, Mary used her considerable strength to push the car back upright. She walked around it and collected the ten wolves she'd taken down; the pelt from their furs would almost make it worth the bother they had caused. She spent the next two hours wrangling the three horses that had escaped the attack. She created a makeshift tether and made it to the convent mostly intact later that night. The Bishop appreciated her dedication and hard work by making her pay out of pocket for the one cracked keg of molasses.

Mary was the perfect example of many of the African-American women who also came to Montana with the first settlers. She also had the drive and strength to claim her freedom and assume non-traditional roles. Not only did she drive a stagecoach, but also held the mail route between Cascade and St. Peter's Mission.

"I woulda told the jerk Bishop to stick it in his ear. He's lucky Mary decided to even continue making supply runs for him. Maybe she got a good price for those wolf pelts," Lauren muttered as she read through her chapter for edits and revisions. "I'm pretty sure if not for the kids; she would've punched him a few times. Though I am surprised she didn't drag him along for the next ride to make sure the molasses keg didn't get broken up."

She stood and stretched. She looked at her laptop, then saved her files and closed it. After a solid three hours of dedicated writing, her work brain was spent. Now she could spend the rest of her day reviewing the time she'd spent with Jared. He'd gone out for work before she'd awoken in the morning, but left a sweet note promising to return about ten and left a carafe of steaming hot coffee for her. Since she had worked up until 9:45 am, Lauren had madly rushed into the bathroom to mix the birds' nest on her head and finger scrub her teeth. Nothing could be done about the wrinkled state of her clothes she'd slept in. She sat at the table, forcing herself to calm down and just drink the coffee.

"Maybe I should take up writing fiction," she said. "No one would believe my car drama is real. Well probably about the crappy rental car, but not the sexy as sin cowboy. Wow… I just said sexy as sin. Maybe I got heat stroke yesterday. Or darkness crazy? I should stop talking to myself."

Her ramblings stopped as she heard a vehicle pull up. She finished her cup of coffee, washed the mug, and put it in the sink. Then tried to figure out if standing or sitting looked more casual. She knew neither would look anything but dorky, so she attempted for not resembling a constipated Muppet as she sat and forced a smile on her face.

"Good morning, Lauren," Jared called as he walked in.

"Good morning, Jared," she returned.

"Let me get you back into town. I'm taking an early lunch," he said.

They'd been on the road for about fifteen minutes, sitting in silence and it made her uncomfortable. The hum of the jeep didn't provide enough distraction. She was used to conversations everywhere, back home. The silence felt odd, though her traveling companion seemed to have no issue with it.

"I'm surprised it takes so long to get back to town. These open spaces are deceptive," she said.

"I also live at the edge of the property," he said. "An hour isn't too bad of a drive. Unless you're renting a car that's determined to make you walk."

"It's better than my last rental car," she said. "The one I had to use in Michigan made sure to make me spill my coffee at every stop. Every single time I had to stop. It had some weird kind hiccup when I pressed the brakes. I had to go shopping for extra blouses. Not having coffee wasn't possible."

"Sounds like air in the brake lines."

"Cowboy and mechanic? You're a jack of all trades," she said.

"Something like that. I like knowing things," he said. "So why were you in Michigan?"

"National conference presentation. I'm a history professor at University of Maryland, and each year they like me to present my research," she said. "Go Testudos!"

"Testudo?" Jared asked.

"They're a genus of tortoises. Funny enough, my cousin Gregory is a testudinologist. He works for For-Mar arboretum and nature preserve in Michigan and gets to drive a Turtlemobile. I really should've visited him the last time I was there."

"A Turtlemobile?"

Lauren laughed at the incredulity in Jared's voice.

"Yes it's a real thing. He drives around to local parks and teaches kids about turtles," she said. "He even makes some lame joke about loving them in all their forms- especially soup. Though I think he stopped after one kid broke into hysterical sobs. It took him almost a half hour to talk the kid down and explain he had been teasing. The parents weren't amused."

"Poor cousin, though I think the joke is funny," Jared said. "And poor kiddo. Although the parents could've just stepped in and made it easier."

"It's why I teach college. I'm just not any good with little ones. They make me really nervous" she said. "They're unpredictable little hormonal time bombs; you never know what will set them off."

"I get you," he said. "My sister has a three year-old, and while I love him, I'm confused at his random behavior switches most of the time. Half the time he's happy and fun, but when something sets him off, his entire life is ruined. This past spring I went home to visit for Easter, and all was going well until he made the connection between chicks and chickens. Dinner was ruined for everyone by his wailing about the dead chickies on the plate. I'm not sure he's ever recovered."

Lauren laughed along with him.

"He tried really hard to convince us eating them was wrong. Funny how chicken nuggets aren't put into the same category yet. I teased my sister she would have to watch and make sure he didn't become an extreme animal activist. And to get therapy money together because those nuggets will be his downfall."

"Yeah, I've had a few students who went that route," she said. "They started off talking about how the vegan lifestyle made for better health. Then they got more dedicated about it and began participating in parades and protests. Then they stepped it up."

"I hope you don't mean they show up at dinner and ruin Easter for you by having a hysterical crying fit," Jared chuckled.

"I wish," Lauren said. "Instead I had to see not one, but three of my graduate students naked."

She began to laugh as Jared turned and gave her a skeptical look, complete with raised eyebrow.

"True story. I was in Oregon for a different work conference two and a half years ago. I had just finished the last panel presentation I had to do and had plans to meet up with friends and explore the city. I tend to treat these conferences as a big reunion because all of my colleagues' jobs are in different states, so I made plans to meet up with my bestie from my grad school cohort for lunch. We sat out on the patio, enjoying one of the few sunny days while we were there. We have a rule about no work chat, since we don't see each other often, instead we were talking about some of the oddities Portland seemed has," she said starting to giggle over the memory.

"Share a few?" Jared asked. "Unless it will wreck the story."

"The Candy Basket boasts the world's largest continual chocolate waterfall. I haven't seen every chocolatefall in the word, but theirs is pretty impressive."

"No hesitation at all to come up with that fact," he grinned. "I kinda hoped it would be something weirder."

"It's chocolate, why would I hesitate? It was the first place I went to see. Weirder, okay, the annual World Naked Bike Ride takes place in Portland each year," Lauren said.

"I think you needed a better segue between those topics. How do we go from candy to nudity?"

"You asked for weirder. It's a seven mile as a protest against dependency on fossil fuels. It also is about bike safety and body positivity. And it's a perfect segue into my story."

"Do tell," he drawled.

"Mina and I were catching up on basic gossip and our lives over the last six months. As we sat there lingering with coffee and dessert, a group of naked people walked by. At first we thought it was just a prank because only a few people walked by and then no one else. However more and more naked people started to walk past us, some had painted messages on their bodies protesting the unethical treatment of animals in the culinary industry," she started to laugh harder, gasping out her story. "We watched in stunned fascination more amazed by their boldness, and then the worst happened. I recognized one of the protestors. At least I did after a double take or two. Funny thing is Chris had always been a quiet introspective person in the classroom; quite frankly one of the last people I could have imagined doing something like that. A few minutes later Oscar, his classmate, went by and just when I thought I was in the clear, my favorite student, Mateo, walked by."

"Surely you aren't the type to play favorites," Jared mocked.

"Not when I grade, but the brain pan on that kid is amazing. Anyhow, he walks by and must've caught the sight of me out his peripheral vision and came back."

The rich laughter rumbling in Jared's chest distracted her from her story. She laughed with him a moment and got back to her tale.

"Not only did Mateo come back and start to chat with me, but he also called Oscar and Chris back to join in on the conversation also," she said. "Thank goodness I'm tall, because my eyes ended up being navel level with the guys. Which was great until Mateo called his fiancée over to meet me, and I met her chest first."

The laughter was contagious and the rest of the ride went much quicker than Lauren wanted it to. She finished her story as Peace came into view.

"I'll send Dunn's out for your rental. I do think you should call the corporate office and get something better brought to you," Jared said.

"Thanks for another ride," she said with a nod. "And thanks for dinner last night. Though I really had meant to treat you. How about a quick lunch?"

"Sounds perfect," he said. "Maybe we should answer a few more questions for each other?"

Lauren felt her pulse jump. She hadn't expected him to say yes. It was the middle of his work day. She grinned as she looked out the window at the small town bustling in the midday. Jared pulled into the parking lot for Sheila's diner. Cars were packed in tight.

"Leftover meatloaf sandwich day," Jared said with a chuckle. "Unless you hate meatloaf with a passion, I'd suggest you try it."

Lauren waited as Jared got out and walked over to open the door for her. From the first time he'd saved her from being stranded, it had been the practice. She actually appreciated it. Her grandfather had opened the door for her every time and it reminded her of her favorite relative in a sweet way.

What Lauren hadn't planned on was every head turning and the conversations quieting as they entered the diner. She didn't hear necks snap as people craned to look at them, but there was no doubt they were looking. A quick frisson of doubt hit her, perhaps interracial couples weren't accepted. But she squashed it as they were led to the back corner booth and reminded herself, they were not a couple- they were having lunch.

"If nothing else, they will get their oblique muscle work out today," Crystal grinned and then squinted at Lauren. "You know about today, right?"

"Leftover meatloaf sandwiches?"

"Okay, I'll be back with yours. By the way, he's never brought a girl here. Nor does he come at lunch time. And he kinda hates meatloaf. That's why they're all staring."

The rapid fire burst of information as the waitress popped her gum and flounced away made Lauren giggle.

"Why are we here if you don't like the menu today?"

"Because the only other place is an hour away, and I do have to get back," Jared said.

"We could have waited until you had time off," she said.

"This is fine," he said with a grin. "I didn't realize my personal life was so fascinating for everyone. I suspect I should pay more attention when the rest of the guys are gossiping. I'm sure they have a lot to say about me."

Crystal returned carrying a platter filled with food. One plate held a large meatloaf sandwich and potato salad and the other with Reuben on rye, two tall glasses of lemonade and two pieces of apple pie. Lauren shook her head at the sheer volume of food. Crystal set the food on the table, slowly, looking back and forth between them. Lauren realized she was waiting for something.

"Tell me about your experiences working with the older generational cowboys, Jared," Lauren asked, hoping to bore the girl away.

It worked and Lauren spent the rest of lunch hearing amazing stories about the men and their families had quietly shaped the structure of the West with little to no recognition. As she finished her sandwich, she realized her book was much more important than she had initially thought. She had a lot of work to do. Her research had just expanded in ways she'd never imagined.

Jared walked her back to the B&B afterwards.

"Thanks for the rescue again," she said and then laughed. "I never thought I would ever say those words."

"My pleasure," he said.

Lauren felt the tension rise and leaned into it. She wasn't disappointed when he met her. The kiss was sweet but brief. When he pulled away, she blushed and couldn't meet his eyes.

"Talk to you later, Lauren," Jared said.

She gave a nervous wave and walked inside and straight up to her room. Fireworks were still going off in her head.

"I kinda expected to do research, not fall for a cowboy," she muttered to herself.

She gave herself a firm mental shake and buried herself in writing for the rest of the day. Lauren definitely need some thinking time.

# Chapter Five

Lauren looked at her notes and sighed in disgust. No new words wanted to come out. She didn't believe in writer's block, but couldn't find the motivation to get started writing again. It didn't help that she'd rather let her mind wander and wonder about Jared instead of writing her text. The kiss had been playing over and again in her mind for last few days. Yes, she'd found him attractive, but getting involved didn't make sense. She had a research to do and then would be returning to the East Coast. Doing a long distance romance hadn't been ever been on her radar. Somehow she couldn't imagine flying back and forth to Montana on a regular basis; especially since she wasn't sure Jared wanted anything more.

*Okay stupid. A kiss doesn't mean a romance. A kiss is a kiss. Maybe it's easy for him since he knows I'm leaving in a week. Or maybe not. Get it together Lauren, it was a kiss.*

She forced herself to bury her phone in her purse and not to text Jared. She didn't have anything other than basic niceties to say to him anyway. From the moment he'd scared her by walking up on her broken car, she'd been fascinated. Not just because he was damn good to look, but there was much more to his story – she could feel it. And the kiss… it had been playing over and over in her mind for the past two days.

*Okay, Lauren. If you get at least one more chapter written, we can text and see what he is up to. The framework needs to be set clearly before we meet with-ummm, what is the librarian's name? Oh yeah, Tish. Oh get real; we know he is working at the ranch with those baby cows. However, once the chapter is done, maybe we can have dinner together. Somewhere not in Peace for privacy's sake. This mental rambling is ridiculous.*

The whole week she'd been in Peace, Lauren learned that ranch time was a real thing. Cowboys didn't just call in sick or take a mental health day off. Work came first, no matter what. She looked at her notes and then grabbed her phone to check her calendar. Her appointment in Cascade with the Librarian Archivist was in two days. She made a mental note to look up the woman's name. She had no good reason not to get the narrative completed about Mary done before she engaged with a bunch of new facts of black cowboys in Montana. While her rudimentary research had laid the groundwork, hearing stories from the families had given her much more. It had adjusted the way she reviewed the written literature because the new information told a more vibrant story.

She had read dozens of books about the American West and the imagery of horseback riding and sharpshooting cowboys; where one in four were African American. Lauren grunted as she went through the database of facts in her head. Popular culture whitewashed the west to erase the huge impact of black cowboys. She hoped her book about Mary would start to set the record straight, if only just a little bit.

Three hours and five thousand words later, she stood and stretched. Once she got focused, the words just flowed. She wanted to grab the rest of her research and go home. She walked down to the kitchen area of the B&B and grabbed some iced tea. Her phone buzzed in her purse as she walked through the door. She managed to put the tea on the table and not sprint to get the phone. She smiled at the text icon.

J: I haven't heard from in a few days. Did you get your chapters written?

L: Yes and a good outline of questions for the librarian in a few days too. Are you done with the baby cows for the day?

J: Not just yet, but I had a break. And what librarian?

L: The one up in Cascade. I have an appointment with her soon. She's been a godsend by compiling archived articles for me to read through. I know it makes me a dork, but I love those old stories.

She paced back and forth in her room and stood in front of the fan for a few moments before she got an answer.

J: Sounds like a fun time. Stories aren't dorky; they tell so much about the culture and climate of an area. More people should enjoy them.

Once again Lauren wrinkled her nose in confusion. Jared claimed to be a just a simple cowboy, but things didn't add up. From all the ranch hands she had interviewed and with all the stories she had listened to, Jared didn't act or speak like a typical cowboy. She couldn't quite put her finger on why he was different, he worked as hard as the other guys, who had nothing but praise for him, but something was just off. Because she dealt in stories for her occupation, she could tell there was much more to him. She planned to ask him the next time they would be alone.

J: Make sure you ask about the American Fur Company too. There were plenty of African American fur traders before they became cowboys. Another line of history you might want to follow.

Lauren stared at her phone and shook her head. He made these little statements, which fit in the context of what her research was about, but always caught her off guard. He knew so much, but claimed to only have a passing interest in history. She finished her tea and sat back in front of the fan. With a sudden burst of needing to work, she opened her laptop and began to write.

Five hours and ninety minutes later she made it out to his small cabin on the ranchlands, picnic basket slung over her arm. She'd paused about two seconds before talking herself into going through with the sudden plan that had come to mind. She walked into the cabin and looked around. She knew it'd be unlocked, but still felt like an intruder. An intruder that was going to feed him, and had good intentions though. She could appreciate the safety in being miles away from anyone else. Her plan sounded sane. Didn't it?

*What am I doing?*

Momentary panic covered her. She wasn't sure if her impulsive idea to bring him dinner actually made sense. She knew he would be home in about thirty minutes, which gave her just enough time to unpack. She put the homey dish of chicken, asparagus, zucchini, herbs and cheese and a creamy risotto in the oven on low. No way she would even pretend to make a steak for him, but rocked at making a spicy chicken showing off her mastery of Asian flavors with chili paste, lime, soy sauce, and sesame oil. A nice bottle of white wine chilled in the ice bucket she'd borrowed and dessert waited on the counter.

Once the table had been set, she lit a candle and hoped he would appreciate her being there. She opened up her journal and began to work, to keep her nerves at bay.

*Mary had a hard life. Yes, she'd managed to escape her life as a slave in Tennessee by escorting the nun and children across the country to Montana but life didn't get easier. She ran her stagecoach the couple hundred miles by herself as she did supply and mail runs in the Old West. And being all alone meant dealing with the lawless lay of the land with just her trusty gun at her side. First were all of the wild creatures waiting for her to fall asleep so they could attempt to eat her, so she learned to make a mean campfire. Of course the huge fire meant she also attracted the murderous lots of gun slinging outlaw bandits. However, just because they murdered people didn't mean they were ignorant. After a few of them got their kneecaps shot out, the rest learned to leave her alone. Mary never had an easy time doing her job, but she was good at it.*

Lauren wished she could use some curse words- even mild ones- like douchebags, in her text. It would be very Mary like. It felt like an insult to write about her ancestors' adventures for a text book and sanitize all the woman had stood for. People wanted to read about the culture, but would bristle at the flavor added via rough language. The woman had multiple run ins with the Sioux Indians until they had worked out a basic "don't attack me and I won't kill your guys" treaty. It felt like a good curse word was warranted. She made a quick note, so she wouldn't completely chicken out about her word choices, and continued to edit.

*Even though her skill with a six-shooter kept most of her problems away, the one thing Mary couldn't out run was the weather. More than once she faced the challenge of a premature untimely death at the hands of the forty degree below zero weather and wind chills which stole her breath. At least as much as it could around her heavy cigar smoke. On a frigid night in February in the 1893 the snow drifts were so thick and densely packed nothing could get through them. Not even Mary. She'd been hauling mail on the route because she'd won the bid and would not allow snow to deter her. She was first African-American woman star route mail carrier which meant she processed posted bonds and proved her ability to finance the route. Fields obtained the star route contract for the delivery of U.S. mail for two four-year contracts, a feat most men couldn't even do. It was during the last year of her contract, she found herself in the situation where the weather screwed her over. The snow piled up so fast the horses couldn't move through it and get to shelter. Mary left the safety of her cart and began walking the horses back and forth with her all night long to keep them alive and warm. With the rise of the sun the next day, she began digging out of the snow piles and eventually made it back up to Cascade, finishing her route.*

"This is a great surprise."

Lauren took a slow breath in to stop the hammering of her heart. She'd immersed herself in the story and hadn't heard Jared walk in.

"I'm glad you like it," she said.

"Did I scare you? You were reading pretty intently."

"You did make my pulse race."

'That sounded like I was flirting,'

Lauren stood and walked over to him, praying she wasn't blushing. She smiled up at him, noting he looked tired. He returned the smile in such a way her face heated up, more. A few more seconds ticked by in silence. She noted Jared had no problem meeting her gaze, like some of the other men. She could spend hours looking into them with no problem.

"I will open this great bottle of wine and we can have a leisurely meal," she offered. "I won't even grill you about cowboys tonight."

He gave a deep belly laugh and nodded.

"I'm going to take a quick shower," he said. "And you can ask me anything you like. Dinner smells amazing."

She took the food from the oven and plated it. She gave herself a solid eight, although she couldn't be held accountable for Jared's questionable taste in tableware. Lauren tried and failed not to giggle like a besotted school girl when she heard the shower stop. She focused on getting everything on the table and not him being naked in the shower. She poured the wine, took a hefty sip, and then refilled her glass.

*Just a casual dinner with a friend. Stop making it awkward with all this rambling nonsense in your head.*

Jared came back out in jeans a t-shirt. Lauren smiled and offered him a glass of wine.

"I made dinner," she said. "I figured it was about time. And since Dunn's let me borrow a reliable car, I'm fairly certain it won't break down and leave me stranded."

She clinked her glass against his, while he chuckled.

"Maybe," she offered. "But I hope not, since I don't have any pages to burn."

"Well, I'm delighted that you're here," he said.

"Delighted?"

"Yes, delighted," he said and moved in closer. "It means feeling or showing great pleasure."

Lauren leaned in the last ten percent and met his lips. While she'd read steamy romances where kisses were described as sizzling or searing, nothing that had prepared her for the explosion of heat suffusing her being. She pressed her hands against his chest to steady herself.

"Yes, that does seem to be the appropriate word," she murmured as she pulled away. "Hungry?"

"Definitely," Jared said.

Lauren knew flirting when she heard it and busied herself with rearranging the plate that was already set. She sat down and smiled up at him. She watched him take a few bites of food, and satisfied that he really was enjoying himself, began to eat herself.

"What's something you like to do the old-fashioned way?"

Her eyes snapped up to meet his. She'd been daydreaming about their kiss again and her face flamed. The logical part of her knew he had no idea what she'd been thinking, but she wondered if she'd made some kind of noise or something.

"Ice cream," she said, proud that her voice didn't shake. "There is something very satisfying about cranking the churn that makes it all the better."

"I agree. Remind me and I'll take you to the Twisty Dip in the next town over. Their ice cream is so good I swear they lace it with cocaine to get people hooked."

"What is something that a ton of people are obsessed with but you just don't get the point of?" she asked as she laughed.

"Snapfiltergram or whatever it's called," he said. "I know people just love their social media, but I just don't understand broadcasting every single moment of your day."

"Right? Not to mention it's like an easy map for any stalker or serial killer to follow," Lauren agreed.

"Do you have firsthand experience with this?" Jared asked.

"No and this is where I have to admit my problem. I love thriller movies, but mostly the old ones. I'm not a huge fan of gore, but I love the psychological ones where the killer tries to mess with their victims' head," she said. "I mostly like them because I try to figure out the plots early on in the film. And then I come up with the best escape plans for all of the situations that happen."

"Have you ever had to use any of your planned escapes?"

"No, but it stands to reason that I don't have to because I have them in place. And with my extra perceptive abilities honed by hours of thriller movies, I don't fall for the tricks and traps. Are you ready for dessert?"

"I am. Would you like me to make some coffee to go with? It looks pretty rich."

"It's chocolate silk pie," she said. "But no coffee for me, I would be up all night if I drank it this late. Besides, the guy at the grocery store told me this wine would pair well with it."

"Wouldn't want to have you up all night... because of coffee."

The slow drawled phrase and deliberate pause raised goosebumps on her arm. She made it to the kitchen and grabbed the pie.

"What have you only recently formed an opinion about?"

"Baby cows."

"What?" she asked bringing the pie to the table.

To her surprise he stood up, took a huge bite of pie and then leaned over and kissed her.

"My recently formed opinion is that right now, I hate baby cows. Especially ones that get lost during my special date dinner," he said. "I'm sorry, Lauren, but I've gotta go. You are more than welcome to stay; however, I don't know how long I'm going to be gone."

"Baby cows indeed," she said. "Actually, if you'll walk me to my car, I'll go back to the B&B tonight. Maybe we have a do over in a few nights?"

# Chapter Six

"Aside from having a fierce reputation from using her shotgun to deter wolves from making a midnight snack out of her, Stagecoach Mary also made it a point to confront and take on the racial power dynamics and gender inequality in Cascade head on. Mary had a passion for cigars and walked around town with one clamped between her lips all the time. Of course the fine menfolk of the town had an issue with her; and in true cowardly fashion decided women were too soft and delicate to smoke them, which meant no one would sell cigars or tobacco to her. Instead of going without, she made her own and made it a point to smoke her homemade cigars in the saloons around town. She gleefully offered to sell some of her home blend to the local men, who figured if she could handle it, so could they; and promptly lost their stomach from the first taste."

Lauren began to giggle after reading her latest passage out loud. She'd picked up the habit of verbal dictation for revising in grad school, and yet was still amazed at how many errors she found. Despite all of her historical research, she had a hard time getting her head around people who figured skin color and gender made someone less able. The more she wrote about Mary, the more she found she really admired the woman. It was one thing to escape slavery; and completely another thing to go ahead and live a life according to her own rules and desires.

"I might have to break some of the normal writing guidelines with this text. I'm writing about a black woman who refused to bow to the rules, just on the principle of non-compliance. Stagecoach Mary sure didn't let other people tell her what to do, and being her great-great-great granddaughter I shouldn't either. Who else gets permission from the mayor of a town to go drink in a saloon when the only other women there were prostitutes? Perhaps my problem is I've been following all of the rules for too long. I mean, what's the worst that could happen if I said no to being on a committee or actually took a sick day when I was sick? This woman had a lifelong pass to break the rules given to her. There is no way I'm writing this book without her flavor shown, it would be a slap in the face and against everything she worked and stood for."

Lauren smiled as she read through the rest of her notes, adding in flavorful words here and there. She felt much better using the raw terms in describing her ancestor, it felt more real and tied to the woman as she wrote about her. It only seemed apropos she not only should, but would describe Mary by breaking the standard rules. Understanding rhetoric meant taking chances, even though the editor of the University Press would undoubtedly frown. But she felt competent to make her case. The worst-case scenario being a revise and resubmit sterilizing her work, but even then she had options.

"Okay, read this last segment and we can see what this man is up to," she promised herself.

Lauren had gotten a few texts from Jared during the last few days, but lost baby cows had been just the start of his job needing his attention. While he really didn't go into great details about all of the things going on, she knew it all the cowhands had been called up. Crystal from the diner had spent almost the entire hour of her lunch filling her in on how summer time at a ranch meant lots of what could go wrong or need repair, often did go wrong. The men pulled many long days without breaks.

"Mary had the habit of never backing down from a challenge. Any time some asshole messed with her, she made him pay. Again breaking the norm she took her own brand of justice in hand, and no one dared tell her she couldn't do what she wished. In fact, instead of receiving the usual atrocities visited upon Black people who stepped outside their rights of the colored lines, the Great Falls Examiner had deemed her the person who'd broken the most noses in Montana. Whether to warn others away or to give her, her due honors, no one really knew. The article ran in the daily after yet another conflict when a man took offense to her for whatever reason and made a rude comment about her femininity as she walked out of a saloon. Mary bided her time to set things right. When the guy stumbled out into the street in a drunken stupor he caught sight of her and offered to make a real woman out of her. She looked at him for a second, said nothing. He leered at her, but before he could say anything else she scooped up a huge rock off the street and gave him a lesson in manners, as she bludgeoned him on the head until other cowboys stepped in and restrained her. This was just one reason nobody ever debated the claim."

Lauren smiled, her work was not just fascinating, but she was done and could now see about finding out what Jared had been up to. The thing she had found best about Peace was her ability to get her work done. She'd finally gotten a rental car that worked and had her appointment up in Cascade the next day. She'd had the leisure time to write without any other pressing issues. The grant covered her extended stay at the B&B, where she'd been given the pity discount for being stranded. Other than Jared as a distraction, she'd been productive like she had been in grad school. She was amazed at the renewal of her vigor and excitement for what she did. Not just in researching Mary, but having the conversations with the men had been eye opening. Having those ties to the past and being able to hear the stories had satisfied her soul. Her phone buzzed and shook her from her reverie.

J: Just a quick check in to say hi. I'm finishing up late tonight. The good news is that I've got the next two days off. I plan to make up for our interrupted dinner date. Talk to you tomorrow.

It hadn't been the news Lauren wanted to read, but she had something to look forward to. She looked around and tried to figure out how to spend the rest of her day. The one thing that had been consistent in her visit had been the scorching hot temperatures. She ended up spending more time inside the small businesses in Peace. She already was a regular fixture at Sheila's diner at lunch time; though she had ventured over to Generic Eric's Sandwich Shoppe and Soda fountain.

True to the name the place made soda the old fashioned way. She watched fascinated as the soda jerk pumped a rich chocolately syrup into a tall glass. She learned the title jerk came from the quick jerking motion of pulling on the handle to add a stream of acid phosphate. After a quick stir more seltzer water was added and the drink served to her with a cherry on top as a flourish. Lauren had expected a good soda, but hadn't expected the enhanced tangy taste and quality of the fizz. It did a good job of ruining regular soda forever for her.

The little space had the small town feel Lauren was beginning to appreciate. The teen population spent plenty of time hanging out at the shop. She quietly observed them just being kids; she knew there had to be plenty of stories she didn't know, but it just seemed so easy for them. Everyone seemed to know each other. People always asked after each other and their families. Of course, it also meant tons of gossip flew around and Lauren heard stories that made her quietly laugh. She waited with bated breath to hear some goodies about Jared. To her dismay no one said anything. Of course she realized a bit later that she would also be attached to the gossip and they weren't rude enough to make comments with her sitting there.

Lauren had never thought exploring small towns in America would have been such an adventure. She'd been fortunate enough to be able to travel to Europe, Greece and South America doing presentations about her work. She ruefully reflected most of her life had been wrapped around her studies and work. An inkling of a thought began to wind through her mind. Perhaps she should take time off? This research trip had been amazing, not just in terms of the stories she had heard, and experiences she'd lived - car drama aside; but more for the fulfillment. Not just meeting Jared, though he'd been a sweet surprise, but the people of Peace overall. She bit back a laugh; she'd checked in with her mentor, Vince, earlier that morning and talked with about all of the craziness comprising her trip.

"The place is called Peace?" he chortled. "Sounds like a tourist trap. Or the setting for a really bad porn movie."

"You know, Vince, not everything is about sex," she snorted back.

"If you're living your life to the fullest it should be," he said. "You know my motto …"

"Yes, I do," she said. "Work hard and play hard."

"And yet, you only listen to part of my advice," he said.

"Not true," she countered. "I went after the grant, although I'm thinking I should've asked for more. I could've got a better car."

"And never met your cowboy, who by the way is the reason you got access to all of those amazing stories.

"Wait, what? This sounds suspiciously like you think it was destiny."

"I'll call it destiny if you come back glowing," he said.

"And with that I'm hanging up," Lauren said. "I'm still waiting for your feedback on the first chapters."

She hung up before he could make any retort. When she had been a fresh faced grad student, she had gotten a bit of culture shock – her advisers and mentors were pretty human; the variety with colorful language habits. Lauren had quickly learned to enjoy the occasional shocks from the amazing scholars she worked with. Peals of laughter broke the memory trance; a small child had apparently had her first taste of soda and giggled because of all the bubbles going up her nose.

"Truth kid," Lauren said quietly, standing. "Nothing will ever be as carbonated as this freshness."

She walked back to the bed and breakfast looking around at their normal and her vacation. In the beginning it had wracked her nerves, all of the greetings and casual conversations stopping her as she walked around. Even Mrs. Carmichael had learned her preference of breakfast foods and Lauren had never felt as pampered with all of the carby goodness making up her plate each morning. Quite frankly it had been the best research project she'd done so far. All of the stories from the current cowboys about their ancestors, all of the stories about her own cowboy ancestors, and all of the bonus stories from the townspeople. As a historian she engaged with texts most of the time, so this ethnographic deep dive had been special.

****

A buzzing sound nagged Lauren out of the most perfect dream of riding off into the sunset. Cliché, true, but she smiled as the scenes left waking mind. She dressed, after a brief shower, and walked down to the dining area. Per usual, the area was empty; Lauren kept odd writing hours and missed contact with the other guests. She didn't really mind, everyone else were paired couples having a vacation. She caught glimpses of gushy displays every now and again; she didn't quite retch in public, but she didn't want to see it either.

After her breakfast, she gathered up her laptop and notebook. She tried not to skip all the way out the door, but found it difficult since she had a date. She almost tripped down the stairs when she saw Jared, casually leaning against his jeep. He looked like a poster perfect model, smoldering look and all. Lauren lost all or her words as he crooked his finger, urging her closer.

"Given your current track record with vehicles," he drawled low and slow. "I figured it would be a much better idea just to escort up to Cascade, rather than having to come and rescue you a few miles up the road. Or, more likely having to hunt you down as you walk off in the wrong direction and get lost on open land again."

She paused on the last step and placed her hand on her hip. She exaggerated a stern look and stared him down. She made a silent prayer as she took measured steps toward him and leaned in close.

"And here I thought manners were a big thing out here in the Wild West. Apparently someone forgot to give you the memo."

She leaned back and crossed her arms over her chest. He crooked his finger again and Lauren gave him her best "I'm not impressed with you" stare. At least she thought it was, because her heart hammered so hard in her chest, she could hear it. Her not giving in and moving toward him had less to do with her strength of character and more to do with the complete disrupt between her brain and her legs. Jared didn't seem to have the same problem, and he crossed the space between them before she could blink.

"So sorry ma'am. My unfortunate east coast upbringing may have hampered my good intentions," he said, the drawl even more pronounced. "Perhaps you could find it within the goodness of your heart to forgive me? I only meant to ensure a safe ride up to your appointment. No disrespect intended."

Somewhere in her brain, she would have rather had him show her an apology in a purely physical well. Her appointment could be damned if he followed through on the promise made by his body language. Lauren swallowed twice before her voice decided to work. She prayed she wouldn't squeak.

"I suppose I might find some forgiveness, if you can get me to Cascade."

She was super proud of how strong her voice sounded. No stutters or random pitch changes to betray her. She'd read the bodice rippers with pirates and lace flying all over. For the first time in her life, she understood the urge to fling herself against another person. She wanted to wrap her arms around his neck and kiss him until she couldn't breathe. She could imagine feeling the tight cords of his arm muscles and running her fingers down…

"Shall we go?"

She may or may not have sounded like a cartoon mouse, but she didn't care and scurried toward the jeep. Never once would Lauren deny being attracted to Jared, but she didn't expect her imagination to freak out on her.

'I am going home next week. I am not having a long distance relationship. Good gravy, get a grip, you don't even have a relationship with this man.'

She mentally chastised herself as she climbed into the jeep and buckled herself in. Jared got in next to her and she felt the casual wink all the way down her spine with a shiver. The man knew how to flirt and then some. He'd turned the heat up from their previous interactions. Lauren didn't quite know what how to respond. Her style didn't include casual flings.

'Although…There's nothing wrong with flirting. And kissing, definitely nothing wrong with kissing Jared.'

The humming of the tires against the road drew her out of her internal thoughts. Jared had said nothing and she'd been so introspective, she didn't know if he had been watching her or not. A small smile playing over his lips made her think he had.

"Thank you," she said. "Even though it is a self-serving move. I do appreciate the ride."

# The Philosophy of Peace

His laughter led to her own and a gentle warmth replaced the heated sexual tension. Lauren missed it just a bit, but knew she had to get her head ready for the information exchange at the library. She settled back and enjoyed the quiet conversation up to her appointment.

# *Chapter Seven*

Lauren stared at the letter in her hand. She wasn't sure how to deal with the information she held. She'd been surprised to find mail waiting for her when she went down for breakfast. It had been overnighted to her. She pulled open the tab to the heavy envelope and found a thick pile of papers. She leafed through and found more information the librarian had promised her. A neon blue sticky note was on the top page.

Dear Dr. Stage,

Thanks for coming in for your visit to MSU; it was my pleasure to show you around. I hope the archives gave you enough information about Mary and the cowboys. It's really exciting to know you got to research an ancestor- especially one with such a rich history here. Learning about all the African Americans holding political office after the civil war was fascinating too; your knowledge is impressive. I have a deep appreciation for your work and bringing to light our history. It pains me how quickly it can be erased.

Here are a few more articles I found about landowners and title claims after more digging. Hope they help. I've also reached out to some of my colleagues, and will let you know if anything more can be found.

On a side note, I think it's great to see you're working with Dr. Baker. I haven't seen anything published by him in a while. I did see him present at a conference a few years ago. You two collaborating on this topic is amazing. I'm sure the intersection between prospectors and African American cowboys will make a great article soon.

Let me know if I can help more.

Ra'Ven

Even though she'd read the letter four times, her brain kept refusing to believe it. Of course an easily verified answer was as close as her cell phone and a search engine. She stared at a grainy picture of Jared and looked over his impressive CV. His research centered around the Old Wild West – he'd researched the Desert Land Act and the impact of settlers on the indigenous Native American living in the area. From the papers he'd written, the man was brilliant; his dropped comments and insight made much more sense to her.

*Dr. Baker? Why didn't he say something? Not that we've had more than a handful of dates. And true I am leaving next week. But why wouldn't he tell me he was an academic too? I shouldn't pry, he must have a reason for not saying anything.*

Laurens' brain immediately jumped to the worst case scenario where he was married with three kids. Then spent the next ten minutes coming up with every excuse possible ranging from him abusing her trust to him being an undercover spy. Then jumped to him using her as a summer fling.

*A couple of kisses don't mean a fling. I don't think he's the type to be a cheater. Then again, I don't know much about him.*

She snorted at herself.

*Why then?*

The question hung in the air. Lauren checked the time, again. They had plans to meet at the Toppin's Bar before heading over to watch the Founders Day All night movie marathon at the drive in theater, appropriately, all cowboy comedies. She flirted with the idea of picking up dinner so they could talk in private, but decided again, not to invade his privacy. While she wanted to have all the answers immediately, she wasn't sure she would get them. In fact she had a bad feeling that bringing up his past might cause problems between them. She wanted her last few days with him peaceful.

'Get back to work. It will make the time go by faster,' she chided herself. 'One full chapter and you can go back to being obsessive about this detail Jared just forgot to mention.'

She threw herself into a writing frenzy. Lauren forced herself to focus on getting her words down on the page. She read through the new articles, annotating and using mini sticky notes to give her a quick visual reference. The material Ra'Ven had provided her with gave more details about the financial strife of African American cowboys and the struggle they had as the experts with no power. After she gleaned all the material she could from the articles, she changed over to her new favorite topic. Lauren idly wondered how difficult it would be to get a movie made about Mary. With all of the independent networks and specialty streaming stations, she might just have a chance at getting it made. Perhaps she could find another grant or funding source. With the new idea in mind, she went back to writing.

*Because of all the run-ins with the local men and Bishop at the nunnery, Mary found herself out of work and with no prospects. She just couldn't find work, but of course she didn't wait for someone's pity. Mary opened two restaurants in Cascade. She didn't care about her inability to cook anything tasty. She went right ahead with her plans for her new line of work. The creation of these restaurants also gave people a glimpse to a side of the powerful woman most had not seen. Compassion. Most knew her kickass nature, but few had ever seen her care. They got to see this when both restaurants failed because she without hesitation gave out free meals to those who needed food in the town. Not surprising, no one even tried to help her succeed with her endeavors.*

Lauren chewed her bottom lip as she read through the next segments. She'd already mentioned some of Mary's work with the United States Postal Service, but with the new set of articles she'd gotten; even more information had been unearthed from the local news posts from the 1890's.

"I suppose I can rearrange the chapter," she groused at herself. "Nothing like a lengthy manuscript overhaul to interrupt all the great work I've done. I wonder if this can be done more memoir style, as long as I'm going to take some risks I might as well introduce the idea of segmenting this textbook into vignette style reads."

*Let's revisit Mary, by looking at her experiences delivering mail throughout the Montana Territory. In 1895, she applied for a job with the United States Postal Service, because she had no other job opportunities or options. Trying to get a position delivering the mail on a postal route in 1880's required an interview like no other. When she arrived, she found herself to be the only woman there, with a bunch of a dozen or so sun worn and grizzled cowboys. Being no spring chicken at the age of sixty, she knew she had to make an impact. The interview was to hitch a team of six horses to a stagecoach as quickly as possible.*

*Rumor has it Mary Fields did it with her flair for style. The first thing she did was look over the three team animals, moving them into different positions to make sure they matched in size in their lineup. Having the essential knowledge allowed her to arrange the animals so the two nearest the coach or any wagon called the Wheelers, were always the largest, strongest horses available, because they were the ones who actually turned the front wheels. The second set of team animals was called the Swing team, and the last team called the Lead, were natural leaders and tended to be smaller and more agile. She sauntered over to the animals, said quiet words in their ears, and charmed them into standing docile while she adjusted each harness to fit just right. She made sure her animals wouldn't get a sore spot from a poorly kept or twisted harness. Once she had the animals hitched and the reins looped and ready near the seat, she went over to the nearest saloon, had a few shots of whiskey and came back to watch the others finish. She leaned up against a post and smoked her cigar and became the second woman – and the first black person of any gender – to work for the United States Post Office.*

*For the next six years, Mary Fields rode a stagecoach packed with money and expensive parcels through the territories delivering mail. It not only takes a tremendous amount of skill to drive a stagecoach through the inhospitable terrain, but a considerable amount of human strength and stamina. The reigns weighed approximately 40 pounds and held three lines per hand. Even though each team was communicated with at separate times; and required separate navigation through their reins, Mary kept tight control. And if the weather made delivery impossible with a team, she would grab the mail bag and walk the route; ensuring the mail on her routes were never late.*

*It was doing this job where Stagecoach Mary earned her nickname and became the legend who smoked cigars, brandished, her trusty shotgun, a pet eagle, and a mule named Moses*

A knock on her door made her look up. Her neck cracked and popped as she stretched as she stood. The stiffness in her legs told her hours had passed. She knew she'd sat too long. Lauren answered the door with a smile.

"We should go before we miss the bull riding contest," Jared said with a smile.

She met his kiss and all thoughts of questioning what she had learned melted away. They could have a discussion later. Maybe going out and having a good time would make him easier to ask. She smiled at him.

"Are you going to ride?" she asked.

"If you will," he teased.

"Sure," Lauren said. "Might as well try new things while I'm here."

Bull riding lasted four seconds for her and seven for Jared. She had been scared and the bull tossed her off on the down dip. Jared had done great until she gave him a lascivious smile and wink. He tumbled to the ground and shook his head. She knew she'd gotten to him and clapped loudly without shame. He came back to where they sat.

"Happy now?"

"Absolutely, I sure didn't want you to shame me by being a perfect rider.

She looked over at Jared, and mentally shook her head. They'd had a few dates, but it certainly didn't warrant her picking up and moving. Especially since there was the little matter of his real identity to discuss. Lauren wasn't sure she should broach it with him. He probably was there gathering research like her, and he certainly hadn't been obligated to tell her. But she figured he might've mentioned something, considering he knew she was on a research sabbatical. They walked hand in hand back to her bed and breakfast. She sadly recognized she would be leaving soon.

Lauren leaned up on tip toes and kissed him. Softly at first, she'd meant it to say goodbye. As his lips pressed against her and their bodies connected passion erupted and engulfed her. She knew she'd be leaving soon and would make him no promises. She bent her rules on casual relationships, knowing she consented with all her being. She didn't see the harm of letting the night naturally conclude.

"Do you want to come up?" Lauren asked. "Have a glass of tea or something?"

She smiled as he nodded and opened the door. The bed and breakfast was quiet; mostly because the other occupants were still out enjoying the pre-celebration events. Despite the excitement, she'd been ready to leave early, though watching the fireworks from the porch had been worth it. They quietly walked up the stairs and made it to her room.

She leaned back into him and kissed him again. His roughened fingers left a trail of goosebumps in their wake as he trailed them over her shoulder. Lauren appreciated the gauzy dress and its lack of coverage as he teased her with his touch. She closed her eyes as he replaced his caresses with small kisses. She shivered and looked into his eyes.

"I'll be right back," she said.

Lauren cursed her bladder for interrupting perfectly good foreplay. Had she even imagined the ending her night had taken, she might've forgone the slushie. And Jell-O shots. And probably *Granny's Gooseberry Tea*. She walked back out and noticed everything had changed. Jared stood in a tense posture, giving her a look

Lauren stared back at Jared, not able to read his expression. He held up a piece of paper. She recognized the University seal, meaning he'd found Ra'Ven's letter. His eyes questioned her, but no sound left his lips. She didn't know how to read the rise in tension, but it didn't feel like a good thing. She gave a small terse smile and raised an eyebrow. His steely gaze surprised her and her spine stiffened. He had invaded her privacy, not the other way around.

"What's up?" she asked.

"I saw this. I wasn't snooping- it was just out on the table," he said.

She didn't like his accusatory tone. She tried to reason that it would be shocking to see her name on a document, but again, he'd looked. Lauren decided just to jump in and try to figure out why things had gotten so tense.

"Why didn't you ever tell me?" she asked. "After all the time I spent talking about my research? After all of the help you gave me? You could've let me know."

"Because I didn't see the point," he said. "I'm sure it may sound odd to you, but I don't want everyone here to know about me."

"Are you undercover gathering research?" she asked bewildered. "I can't imagine why you wouldn't want people to know. Not for nothing Jared, the librarian in Cascade recognized you easily enough. Information is easy to find on the internet. Why are you trying to hide your accomplishment?"

"It's a title, Lauren. Nothing more. And quite frankly, with all I'm going through, it doesn't mean a whole bunch. I'm just Jared the ranch hand, not W. Jared Baker, the scholar. Not anymore."

Lauren's head spun. Getting her doctorate had taken six years of research, classes, presentations, publications and dealing with departmental politics. It also was the culmination of a lot of hard work and effort toward success. While she'd had good and bad experiences, nothing she could imagine would make her walk away from it all.

"What are you doing here?"

"I'm working on my cousin's ranch. After years in Academia, the physical labor is quite rewarding. I do my job, do it well and get a good night's rest. The cows rarely talk back and I'm allowed to just be."

Lauren wanted to ask many more questions, but bit her tongue. He didn't owe her any answers. Despite finding out about him also being PhD was shocking; it wasn't a crime. She'd known the man all of a few weeks and all he'd ever done was show her respect and help her out. Somehow pressing him about a personal decision didn't seem fair. Then again, he'd looked at a private letter.

"I don't buy it, you don't just walk away from your research without a good reason," she insisted.

"You do when your mentor steals your work from under you and publishes the findings."

# The Philosophy of Peace

The words dripped bitter from his lips and she stared at him in shock. Of course she'd heard the stories about these kinds of things happening in the academic community. In fact, quite a few of her friends had warned her again work with a well-known but notoriously thieving scholar, Ellen, who often befriended African American students and then stole their work. She tried to justify it by telling anyone who would listen how she was giving students of color a boost to their careers. Meanwhile she cost more than one their publication rights. Lauren sighed. Apparently the practice was wide spread.

"But you're his peer," she said.

"Not when you're on the tenure track you're not," Jared said. "I thought I'd found the perfect job. I got to continue my research at a major university. I admit I had been star struck to think of working with such a giant in the field. It just took me a while to figure out he considered my work an extension of his own. Anyhow, I'd made a great connection between prospectors and a trail of diseases. I spent a week in a writing frenzy and put together what would be the penultimate chapter on my first book. I sent it to him in an email, proud of what I'd done and waiting for him to praise me as well. And I heard nothing for three months."

She watched Jared begin to pace and felt for him, the memories obviously still pained him.

"I only found out about what he'd done when a friend of mine, who had beta read for me, called to ask my why I'd given my mentor my chapter to publish instead of publishing it myself. In the months he'd been out of contact, he'd gotten the article published in a journal and already done a conference presentation showing off the work," Jared said in a low voice.

Lauren sat down; she knew how hard he had worked gathering information, double checking sources and finally get it written down. Getting published was an accomplishment because of the rigor in writing and revising that often had to be done. But a conference presentation? That was the showcase to let your peers know what you were working with and stake a strong claim. She could feel his frustration and sorrow.

"Even worse, once I started pressing back, showing the Dean of our department my emails as proof of my work, I got slapped down. After I presented all of my complaints, he thought about it for only a moment. He then explained to me, quietly but loudly enough for the rest of the office to hear, his doubts about my claims. He questioned my respect for my mentor and flat out asked me if I was trying to claim more of the work than I should."

Lauren shook her head as she heard his story. Despite having been warned off from certainly faculty members, she hadn't realized that Jared might've had the same experience. Somehow she figured it would've been different for a white man. She sat and listened to the rest of his story. The Dean accused him of refusing to follow any of his mentor's advice regarding research topics and how to set it up. The mentor had claimed, early on, he had tried to work with Jared closely to cultivate the topic, but had all help refused.

"It just killed me. Here I am working day and night to put this research together, to make a great chapter for my book. For months I pondered and stressed on a daily basis if I did justice to the data, and more importantly, to the people whom I represent through that data," he said. "I hope you never have to understand. Good night Lauren."

# Chapter Eight

Lauren sat on the sofa staring at the bustle on the street. She wanted to talk to Jared and say her piece, but also understood he was understandably upset. She couldn't even fault him for reading the letter; she'd left it out in the open. Of course she hadn't expected for him every to see her room.

**J: Are you awake? I don't like how I left last night. Give me just a quick chance to explain?**

**L: Yes. Where would you like to meet?**

**J: There is a gazebo at McBride Memorial Park. It's only a five minute walk from you. See you soon.**

Lauren stood and blew out a nervous breath. One the one hand she was glad he hadn't refused to have the conversation. But there was also the possibility it might be bad. Her brain oscillated between things going well and Armageddon during the brief walk. She found him standing in the center of the gazebo and walked right up to him.

"I've been thinking," Jared said softly. "I owe you an apology. I shouldn't have snooped."

"The apology should be from me. You're right; I have no idea what you went through. I'm sorry your trust was betrayed."

"I have a lot of decisions to make and soon. I was terse because my sabbatical is coming to an end soon. I either have to go back to UConn and pretend I can work with those people, or I can go back onto the job market. And then I could just stay here a while longer, or at least I thought so. Just being around you doing research, has reminded what I really love to do. What I'm missing," he said.

Lauren shook her head, she couldn't imagine his decision.

"Can I offer my two cents?" she asked.

"Sure," he said.

"If you're going to end up staying here, you might as well fight. The majority of stories that I've heard about scholars having their work stolen have been from women and scholars of color.

You taking a stand will speak pretty loud," she said. "It won't be us playing the color card; it won't be a claim of being a hysterical female. You could help change things for the better.

She waited while he pondered her words. She had asked a lot of him. The backlash from the academic community could be brutal. The university could refuse to acknowledge the claim, ending in a costly court battle. Or his department could decide to support his mentor. He might possibly never be hired again. Lauren understood what was at stake. She just hoped he would really think about what she'd said.

"I'm going to sleep on it," he said after a long pause. "One of the best things I learned being out here and working with the animals, is sometimes you have to be well rested before you make a serious decision."

They walked back to the bed and breakfast in silence, but not a stifled one. As they reached Main Street a vendor walked by and offered them a peach tea slushie, which they happily accepted. They sat on the porch swing and chatted; the vendor came back by to offer more slushies. Exchanges of childhood stories, grad school mishaps, and even an embarrassing holiday festive story or two rounded out their evening. She again met Jared as he leaned in and shared a slushie flavored sweet kiss.

****

Lauren woke to shrieks. Not the kind that induced panic because someone was being eaten by a bear; those would've been quieter. Instead they were joyful, at least to the sound maker she assumed. After having stayed up to work on her manuscript, she would've happily locked the child in a box. She rolled over and blinded herself with her phone screen as she tried to get a fix on the time.

'Nine in the morning? What can be so shriek worthy? It's not even noon. I can't imagine why children should be able to make sounds so high pitched if not in danger. Maybe he is being eaten by a bear?'

She sat up in bed and waited to feel slightly more awake. A gentle knock sounded at the door.

"I've brought you a tray, dear. Coffee and muffins to get you started. I'm going to get ready for the parade. Just leave the dishes in the sink."

"Thank you Mrs. Carmichael," Lauren said as she grabbed her robe.

She poured a cup, and didn't mind the slight sting she got from trying to drink the steaming hot coffee. Grabbing the carafe, she went over to her, now usual, seat on the sofa. She peered out the window in awe. The normal streets of Peace had undergone a radical transformation. Banners were hung from every street light pole proudly stamped *Peace Founder's Day Celebration*. Main street was lined with brightly colored tents, balloon and ice cream vendors already walked around hawking their wares.

With everything going on, she'd forgotten the Founder's Day Celebration parade would run at nine am that morning. Of course, it was because her head was pounding and slightly fuzzy from the slushies she'd drank the night before. Lauren didn't know if she'd be ready to enjoy the impending festivities, but no matter at this point. Clearly they had started in full force. She laughed at her lack of observational powers, though the town had been dark and fairly quiet when she and Jared had less conversations bits and more yawns. She'd gotten armed with a ton of new information about Mary as well as other African American cowboys; even better yet she's started to figure out the puzzle which was Jared Baker. Sipping her coffee as she watched small children finagle their parents into cotton candy and funnel cakes for breakfast. There were people walking up and down the street, but it looked like the festivities had just begun to start. She shamelessly gawked and people watched while she ate her muffins, fruit and egg cup.

If nothing else, she would really miss the breakfasts from the B&B. They were always full of flavor and managed to hit the spot. Lauren doubted coffee would ever be a substantial enough breakfast again. It made her sad to think she would be leaving in a few days. Her phone buzzed.

**J: Can you be ready in ten minutes?**

**L: Ready to see you? Or ready to be seen in public?**

**J: Okay, fifteen minutes, but no longer. And yes, in public. It's a surprise, go with it.**

Lauren didn't answer; instead she fought her way into her robe and prayed no one was in the shower down the hall. The luck- gods of the shower were with her, the bathroom stood empty and the hot water flowed until she finished rinsing her hair. Twisting her hair and wrapping it into a top-knot proved to be the fastest choice. However, clothes stopped her short. She stood in her undies trying to decide the less of two evils. She had a business casual set of slacks to pair mock turtle neck sleeveless light sweater and a business casual skirt paired with a puffed sleeve blouse. She had thrown clothes into her suitcase without thinking she would need anything other than work attire. Her plans for her trip to Montana had been work driven. She pulled out both outfits to figure out which was the least offensive, when static cling saved the day.

When she pulled out her skirt, a trail of ombre colored fabric came out with it. Lauren stared at the sunset blush pink, cream, and light blue dip-dye maxi dress. The material was thin and breezy with a drawstring apron neckline with front and back cutouts. The dress was sleeveless with high slits up either side of the legs in the full skirt. And returning the stupid thing had been on her to-do list for the last two weeks. She'd been shopping for new slacks for work. Her problem with being slightly taller than average meant her waistline almost always gaped if they leg length fit. Nice long legs, nice tiny waist, and full derriere equaled always having her clothes tailored. She'd grabbed four pair of sensible, but comfortable slacks in various muted colors and tossed them on the counter. The cashier looked about twelve years old and extremely nervous. The transaction had taken a full twenty minutes, and Lauren hadn't bothered to check the receipt.

When she got home she found the dress and cursed for a full two minutes. It wasn't her style, way too thin, too revealing, and she certainly never wore rayon. However, at the current moment, the accidental purchase had been arranged by angels. It fit her perfectly; the side slits stopped just short of too much exposure up her thigh and the color glowed against her skin. She let her hair out of the knot, sprayed on some lavender essential oil blend and opened the door at first knock.

"Hi," she said pulling the door open.

"So glad I gave you fifteen minutes," Jared said.

"Give me three more?" she asked.

Lauren sat on the edge of the bed to put on her sandals rather than risk toppling over doing the flamingo routine. She caught him staring when she looked up, and wondered if she'd accidentally flashed him. She began rethinking the sheer dress. She could just wear her regular clothes. But then she'd have to change and explain why.

"I'll be right back," she said.

She firmly closed the bathroom door before brushing her teeth. She stared at herself in the mirror.

"I look fine," she muttered around the brush. "It's going to be hot. The dress is just light, not see through. Mary would wear this and not give a damn,"

Lauren smiled at her reflection. In her last chapter she'd found on her favorite Mary stories so far. Her ancestor lived life on her own terms, but of course people had problems with her. It might've been because she lived hard; she worked hard, drank hard and of course spoke with an endless stream of hard profanity flavored rants. Granted she had a reason. Despite all of her hard work didn't mean much to those who were upset with her living life on her own terms. Her latest round of trouble could've been avoided if Mary had been able to turn the other cheek- like the convent she worked for preached. One day she'd found out the handyman she worked with had an issue with her. He'd been going around Cascade, mostly to the different saloons and whining loudly that Mary made more money than he did. Granted he stayed in the relative safety of the convent and did the work requiring few skills, other than being mostly sober and pushing a broom.

Apparently Mary had as much disdain for his avoidance of a good and easily solvable confrontation, as she did about his claim that a black woman shouldn't make more money than he did. No matter she routinely braved the elements and feral animals; him mucking out the stalls equaled just as much hard work. She didn't agree with the claim or him talking crap about her. She made it a point to find him where he was tucked away in the corner of a saloon, whining to anyone who would listen about the injustices of the world. Mary stood up tall, cracked her neck and met his eyes with a death stare. She challenged him to a duel behind the nunnery. With a crowd around him, he couldn't very well back down. So he followed behind her, trying to gather up local support, which he did, plenty of locals who wanted to see the woman get her due. Mary reached under her apron and pulled out her trusty Smith & Wesson .38 calm as could be. In the next moments of chaos, the whiner found himself in possession of a bullet right in the buttocks, while Mary turned around and went back to work.

While she didn't get harmed from the duel, she did get fired. The Bishop, the one who charged her for the broken barrel of molasses, took offense to her discharging a firearm on the holy ground of a Roman Catholic convent. Mary, being Mary of course, went on to plan B and after a week of her being gone, the Bishop had a stellar freak out when he realized the handyman couldn't bring them supplies.

"I'm pretty sure Mary laughed the entire time," Lauren said.

She rinsed her mouth, straightened the dress down her legs, and walked back to meet Jared.

"I'm ready," she said.

"You're beautiful," he said. "Let's go have fun."

Lauren barely had time to blush because Jared laced his fingers through hers and led her out the door. The warm morning air and bright sunshine made her smile. While she still didn't appreciate the earlier shrieking, she could understand it. The excitement was palpable around them. People milled about everywhere, tons of kids ran to and fro between the booths. It finally dawned on her it had to be a weekend to have this many children around. Her small worry about other people's kids vanished the second the aroma of barbeque filled her nose.

"Wow, that smells amazing," she said.

"Yeah, Oscar was an old pain in the butt, but she will make for some means ribs," Jared said.

"What?" she exclaimed. "Jared, you can't be serious."

"Burgers might be the best part, but I'm sure she'll be tasty no matter what."

Lauren burst into laughter.

"I can't believe you would say that about one of your cows."

"You do know hamburger is chopped cow meat, yes?" he mocked.

"Stop it. Wasn't he like a pet?" she asked.

"No, *she* was a complete pain in the butt. This is why I named her Oscar, like the grouch."

Lauren continued to laugh as they walked by a dozen food booths, and she silently promised to try each one. Especially the one with elephant ears.

Hours passed in a snap and Lauren felt giddy from the amazing day. She'd never imagined, well to be honest, she never could have imagined spending a day at a town faire or Founder's Day as it were. She'd never even gone to a block party at home, so the novelty still amazed her. Everything had been amazing. She stood on the porch of the B&B grinning at Jared.

"I never would have imagined that a Ferris wheel would be so creepy," she said and didn't even mind his laughter. "I mean, it goes so slow, but it freaked me out every time we got to the top. All I could imagine was the basket slipping off of its rusty hinges and plummeting to death."

"That image might just ruin Ferris wheels for me," Jared said.

"Well you can blame George Washington Gale Ferris Jr. He originally designed and constructed the observation wheel for the 1893 World's Columbian Exhibition in Chicago. So he's the one who made it so tall," she said.

"Why do you know that, if you never have been on a Ferris wheel?" Jared asked between laughs.

"I have a penchant for collecting stupid facts, I guess," she said. "I read it once and found it fascinating. It also explains why *Ferris* is always capitalized but wheel isn't."

They watched the fireworks in silence until the end of the impressive display. As Lauren looked around the small town, she could again see the enticement in staying in the area. People actually knew each other and had an investment in the lives of their neighbors. She barely knew the names of the neighbors on either side of her condo; the sense of belonging wasn't the same. Even still, she doubted she could live in such a remote area. She'd been born and raised in metropolitan areas, the quiet was good for research, but she didn't know about the slower pace full time.

She caught Jared starting at her.

"What?" she asked as she moved closer to him.

"Is the offer for the tea still open?" he asked second before capturing her lips.

She waited until she was breathless before standing up, nodding an affirmative, and offering her hand to lead him up to her room.

# Chapter Nine

"Stagecoach Mary retired in 1901and opened a laundry service in Cascade. Even with something as mundane as laundry she couldn't be ordinary. One day Mary, needing to take a break from cleaning other people's clothes, decided to join a high stakes game of poker at her favorite saloon. Hours later, after she'd had a great afternoon drinking whiskey and winning loads of money, she heard a loud voice outside that caught her attention. The men at the table cringed as a scowl crossed her face and she stood up slow and deliberate. The, now 72 year old woman, calmly and politely excused herself from the card table, telling the men to hold the game for just a few moments. She stalked outside to confront the man who stood on the stoop bragging about how he's gotten one over on her. He drunkenly told anyone who would listen about getting his laundry done but not paying his bill. She grabbed the braggart by his shoulder, and as he turned toward her, knocked him backward onto the ground with one well-placed punch. Then she leaned over the guy's crumpled body in the middle of the street and informed him in a slow drawl, the pleasure from busting his face with her fist gave her far more enjoyment than she'd ever get from the two bucks he owed her. As she walked back toward the saloon, she turned and spat at him and told him deal done.

Despite her gruff exterior, Mary was also kind hearted, and so beloved by the town of Cascade when her home burned down in the fire of 1912, everyone in town got together and built her a new one. After a life far more exciting than anything most people will probably ever experience, Stagecoach Mary Fields finally died of liver failure, no doubt because of her penchant for whiskey, in 1914. She'd lived to be 82 – no small feat considering she'd have to fight for her very existence to exist. In the end Mary left a legacy and tale to be told for years to come."

Lauren held her breath as the sound of Jared's voice trailed off. She looked at him, waiting for his next words. She counted to thirty in her head, wondering just how much time he would need before he gave her any feedback. At the seventy-three second count, she raised an eyebrow at him and received a wink back.

"Jared!"

"This is great Lauren," he said with a quick laugh. "Really well done. I'm sure your ancestor would be pleased with your portrayal of her."

The nervous weight fell off her shoulders with his words. She'd never finished writing a book so quickly in her life. The conversations with the men had made it easy for her to put words on the page. After her writing haze wore off, she found the manuscript complete and ready for the first round of edits. She'd been pleased with her read through and asked Jared if he would mind.

Playfully reminding him how he'd asked for a copy of it weeks before. He agreed and taken two whole days to go through it.

"Did you get a sense of her style? Her way of life? Was it too casual?"

"Her personality came through nice and clear, and I think a book about someone this colorful bends the rules of how formal the text should be. It doesn't deter from the serious history lesson. Quite frankly, I think it's high time cultural voices are much more represented and heard."

She wanted to fling her arms around his neck and hug him tight. After deliberating about three seconds, she gave into the urge. Lauren snuggled into his embrace as his arms encircled her. A couple moments later, the bittersweet hit her. She was done with her research on Mary, meaning she would be returning to Maryland. Her small working vacation had given her amazing opportunities.

"Let's go grab a bite for lunch he offered. "Since I had to beg for today off, we should make the most of it."

She shrugged and enjoyed the short walk downtown. The Founder's Day Celebration had ended and the small town had gone back to everyday life. Lauren knew she would miss being there. She'd grown fond of the people and almost used to their chatty nature. They were motivating and really humanized the history lessons she had learned about. She could easily imagine Peace looking pretty much the same as it had, hundreds of years ago. Toppin's bar came into sight.

"One last fresh bison burger before you go," he said.

Lauren had no complaint. Jared made a great burger, but Old Saul the bar cook was far superior. She made a silent promise to come back to Peace a few times for the burgers. They walked into the bar and greeted the few locals already there. Jared ordered their food and led her back to a booth.

"What are your next plans?" he asked.

"I'm pretty sure the next few weeks will be full of revising, editing and fighting to keep the text language as colorful as possible," she laughed. "And then back to the regular grind of classes, committees, and other stuff. What about you?"
"Well, from what I understand this is the time we market the animals, transport sales stock and get general maintenance done," he said. "It will be my first fall run. I came here last November, so this is still new to me."

Lauren was interrupted by the arrival of their food. She lost what she had been going to say as the huge platter of food was set in front of her.

"I didn't want you to go back to your big city without a solid meal," Old Saul drawled out. "And if you ever decide to write a book about Peace, come back. I've got some great personal stories for you."

Lauren had not expected the gently rumbled offer to make tears well up in her eyes. The world she knew worked on the survival of the fittest. While she knew the town had its own share of drama and turmoil, she'd been given the best treatment possible since she'd been there. Not to mention, she'd never had so many people interested in what she did. Over her few weeks there, people had been engaged and offered up many personal stories that brought her content to life. Details and creative descriptions she never would have found just from reading archives. Even though Mary had been from Cascade, the people in Peace were still interested in learning about the woman.

"That is an amazing offer," she said. "I am certain I will be back to take you up on your generous offer."

The older man nodded and shuffled away. Lauren bit back laughter as she heard him mumbling about her "damn Yankee accent" and it throwing him off. She and Jared chatted softly as they finished their lunch. They left the bar and strolled through the town, visiting the last few shops she hadn't gotten around to. His cell rang and he excused himself, while Lauren looked through the second hand shop *Walk-in-Closet*, for a few mementos to take home.

Instead of finding a bunch of figurines to collect dust on her shelves, she found something better. The purchase was made and wrapped before Jared walked back into the store. She could tell, from his posture, something was different, but he said nothing to her. She smiled, for once having a secret of her own.

"Let's get one final soda," Jared said.

"Sure," Lauren agreed.

She embraced each of her lasts. She saw no point in being maudlin on her last day. Lauren had adopted Mary's moxie. Living her life to the fullest while in Montana had been great. She only hoped she would be able to keep some of her newly learned strength when she got back. At the soda shop, she and Jared laughed as the local teens came over and pelted her with questions. She answered as fast as she could.

"Wow," she said, after they'd been left alone. "The drawl must come as they age. I'm glad to know teens are the same, no matter where they are. Speaking of drawls, why don't you sound like me?"

"I didn't need to stand out extra, so I listened and emulated," he said in a very clipped and polished Connecticut accent.

Lauren burst out in laughter.

"Wow, the surprises don't stop with you, do they?"

"Nope," he said. "And with that, I have to leave you for a few hours."

She started to protest, but stopped when he help up his hand.

"We have dinner plans and I won't be late," he promised.

"Baby cows?" she asked.

"Something like that," he said with a grin.

"I'm sure I can find something to do," she said airily.

They shared a quick kiss. She waited until he drove away, before rushing to Sheila's diner.

"Crystal, I need your help."

****

Lauren blew out a nervous breath. Jared had sent her a text to meet at his place for a romantic dinner. She giggled because he'd actually used the words in his text. Like their goodbye dinner would have been any different. She pulled up in the rental car, who'd done her the favor of not breaking down on the way in. She sat in the car a few extra seconds.

"This is stupid," she scolded herself. "Go in there."

She walked over and knocked on the door. Jared opened the door and she appreciated the long silence and stare. At the second hand shop she'd found a lavender lace sheath dress. It hugged against her and with Crystal's help had found a beautician to help with hair and makeup.

"Wow," he said.

"Good response," she said with a wink and pulled him close for a kiss.

"I've got a proposal for you," he said.

She stared at him stunned. Those weren't words she'd expected to hear.

"I wrote a grant proposal and got it," he said quickly. "It funds a year sabbatical for a research team to gather family stories and history. And if you're willing, I want to claim my research. I'll need some support."

Lauren didn't quite believe the words he said. The silence stretched between him. He grinned down at her.

"If you're interested in staying here to do more research and help me out," he said.

"Yes," she said.

And then paused and looked at him.

"Yes. I want to do this project with you. I would love to help you. What grant? How? Why?"

Lauren's head spun. She had a to-do list a mile long. There were details to consider and she'd need to call Vince. She looked up at Jared. She snuggled close when he pulled her in and kissed him. The embrace calmed her racing thoughts.

"We can start getting everything together tomorrow," she said.

"I hoped you'd said that," Jared said. "I have better plans for tonight."

Lauren smiled at him.

"So I get to stay in Peace a while longer," she said. "I think Mary would approve of this adventure."

"I'm pretty sure she would."

Lauren took a deep breath and looked all around before landing her gaze on back on Jared.

"In studying my ancestor I learned an amazing history. I never thought I would get so attached, but I definitely found a new side of myself here. And then you offer me a chance of a life time. I look forward to our next year together," she said.

They kissed again, until Lauren began to giggle.

"What's that?" he asked.

"To think, we met because of a crappy car," she grinned.

"I like to think it was kismet," he said.

"To new adventures," he said handing her a glass of wine.

"To Peace," she said.

Lauren kissed him again, glad for the new opportunity to stay in Peace and explore her new options. Their glasses clinked and a sip of wine was taken, before Lauren put her glass down and kissed him again. She had new passions, research, and vigor for her life. She'd expected to research cowboys, but to her delight she fallen for one.

*** The End ***

# Authors Note

Dear Readers,

Thanks for coming along in this new journey for me.

Many thanks also to Stef and the other amazing Authors who delved into the world of Peace. This has been the most amazing group experience. To have so many women, world-wide, working in the same town and the same universe with common elements has been amazing. The group chat was amazing and everyone was excited to participate. We've all pitched in to make this experience one of a kind. The generosity and love from this group has been the best.

Here's my confession – I loved the idea of doing a group project. So when I was asked to join, I said yes. And had NO idea I would be writing about cowboys. Yeah- I write Fantasy, and the thought of writing a sweet romance minus werewolves was crazy. However the group was too amazing to leave. Instead, I embraced this as a challenge to write in a new genre and style. I delved into researching African American cowboys and much to my delight found out about Mary Fields. Once I started finding out about her- the story came into sharp focus. I did fantasize about a story where Lauren found out that Mary was actually a werewolf, still living and protecting Cascade, but maybe that's for another novella ☺

I hope you all enjoyed the story and will read all of the other great stories from our group!

Best,

Jennifer

# About the Author

Jennifer Fisch- Ferguson has been writing and publishing fantasy stories since 2003. Publishing credits include short fiction, writing contests and novels. She enjoys the freedom of creating new worlds and inviting readers to come along for the ride.

She attended the Eastern Michigan University and graduated with a B.A in African American History and promptly went to work with AmeriCorps on a literary initiative. She went to the University of Michigan and got her Master's degree in Public Administration in 2008 and while she finished writing her thesis, also got a Masters in English – Composition and Rhetoric in 2009. She has her PhD from Michigan State University in the field of Writing and Rhetoric. She has been teaching collegiate and community writing classes since 2003 and loves the variety and inspiration her students bring.

She lives in the Midwest with two amazing sons, one coffee supplying mate and acts as staff-in-residence to four often-mischievous cats.

- See more at: http://AuthorJFF.com